Boys Like Daniel

A Journey of Desire and Reckoning

D.J. Ciccarello

BOYS LIKE DANIEL: A JOURNEY OF DESIRE AND RECKONING

ISBN: 979-8-9898435-9-6 (eBook)

ISBN: 979-8-9994283-0-1 (Paperback)

ISBN: 979-8-9994283-1-8 (Hardcover)

Library of Congress Control Number: 2025914123

For more information, contact: https://www.djciccarello.com

Cover Design by Juan Jose Padron
Proofreading by Dominic Wakeford
Published by D.J. Ciccarello, Atlanta, GA 30328

Recommended for readers ages 16 and up.

Boys Like Daniel is a coming-of-age novel that explores themes of queer identity, emotional reckoning, and intimacy. It contains mature content, including adult language, consensual and non-consensual sexual encounters, and emotionally complex situations. This story is intended for an Upper-YA, New Adult, and Adult audience.

Also by D.J. Ciccarello

Boys Like Kevin

The Lucky Chip

No Time for Duplicity

To David W. Singleton.

My best friend, mentor, and advocate.

"Desire is the kind of thing that eats you and leaves you starving."

—*Nayyirah Waheed*

1

THE MORNING AFTER

(June 1986)

Waking up next to someone used to mean something. At least, that's what I thought. Now, it only means I drank enough not to go home alone.

The ceiling fan clicks with every turn—a sharp, disquieting sound. Sunlight creeps through the blinds, casting shadow bars across the rumpled sheets now twisted around my legs. I stare up at the uneven rotations of the fan blades, willing time to rewind, as if I watch long enough, last night might unravel itself.

The sheets reek of sweat, smoke, and sex, like the club the night before, familiar and forgettable. My head throbs, like it always does the morning after, but it's not the alcohol. It's the emptiness that takes longer to shake. Twenty-four shouldn't feel this used up.

Shifting to free my numb arm wedged beneath a body I don't remember inviting up, Rick—whatever his last name is—stirs beside me, mumbling something into the pillow before stretching and rolling onto his stomach. He flops one arm over the far edge of the bed and looks comfortable. Too comfortable—as if he thinks he belongs here.

It's clear now we ended up back at my apartment: not his place, not the car, not the bathroom at the park like a month ago. No, last night we ended up back here, *my* apartment in 2B, where Daniel Whitmire lives.

I'm careful not to wake him. Not out of kindness but because I'm not ready to talk. Not to him, not about anything. Sitting up, I swing my legs over the edge of the bed. My jeans are crumpled on the floor, as if I stumbled in at 2:00 a.m. and peeled them off half-conscious and in a rush, leaving the mess for the morning. Last night was a repeat of the routine: eye contact, the right half-smile, a drink, then more. Sliding my jeans back on, I wonder when this stopped feeling like freedom and started feeling like a form of forgetting.

Shirtless, I pad to the bathroom, sidestepping the laundry basket and last night's bar shirt. I brush my teeth and splash cold water on my face, avoiding the mirror until I accidentally glance into it out of habit. The reflection stares back with tired eyes and a too-practiced detachment—like nothing touches me—like I'm just passing through.

From the bedroom, Rick stirs and mumbles something that sounds vaguely like my name.

"Don't go back to sleep," I call out. "I'll walk you down."

He sits up, blinking against the light. "Are you always this polite?"

"No," I say, grabbing a clean shirt off the back of a chair. "But it's a building with nosy neighbors."

"Subtle," he says as he dresses, smiling as though last night was more than what it was. He's not my type in the daylight; he's too young, too hopeful.

Moving to the kitchen, I decide not to make coffee. There's no reason to give Rick cause to linger—nor give him any more of myself than I already have. Leaning against the counter, I hear a dog bark outside, a car starting, and the sound of Rick's piss cutting through the surface of the toilet water through the open bathroom door.

The throb of the nightclub's bass is gone. The script played out as expected: the flirtation, the undressing, the cadence of fucking—like an actor hitting all of his marks. Still, some part of me hoped it might feel different this time. It doesn't.

I know what to expect afterward: the disinterest and angst, the clean-up, the new name I won't remember. I don't feel hungover, just hollow, like I spent something I didn't have. It feels like Sunday—another weekend lost and folded into the emptiness of all the ones before it.

He walks into the kitchen, hair tousled, shirt clinging to his chest. "Any coffee?"

"I've got to run some errands," I say. It's not a lie. It's just undefined.

He nods, looking around like the place might tell him who Daniel Whitmire is. It won't. The apartment is sparse: a couch, some records, books I haven't read. There are no photos to cherish, no phone to talk to people, no past to answer for.

"Here," he says, scribbling his number on a receipt from his wallet. "We should hang out again."

It lands in the palm of my hand and then on the counter behind me.

Rick lingers a second, maybe hoping for something more. A kiss? A reason? He gets neither as I walk toward the door to hold it open for him.

Taking the stairs down the three floors to the street, he talks about the club, the music, and meeting me. He says I looked like someone who wasn't there for the music. *Who says I was there at all?* But he's not wrong. Nodding, I let him go on, letting him believe I'm still half-listening.

Outside, he brushes my arm. It barely registers.

"You're not gonna call, are you?"

I meet his eyes. "No."

He submits a small, resigned smile. "Didn't think so," and turns to head to his car.

Humidity curls the ends of my hair, and Midtown moves around me: buses, traffic, people spilling out of the twenty-four-hour nightclub or heading to church in their Sunday best. Both groups worship their chosen salvation: different sanctuaries, yet the same hunger.

I need coffee. Down Juniper, past the florist and bookstore, there's a café near the corner of Piedmont and North Avenue. It's not my usual spot, but something pulls me in that direction. Maybe the wind or the chance to disappear.

Corner Café has open windows and a line of patio tables with umbrellas shimmering under the morning light. I push the door open, and a small bell overhead jangles with forced cheer. The air inside is cooler and smells like cinnamon and over-brewed espresso. I order a black coffee with sugar, then step outside to wait under the awning, still shaking off the effects of last night and the thought of Rick peeing in my bathroom.

That's when I spot them inside the café, across the room, by the windows—two guys at a table in summer clothes. They look too stylish to sweat. The taller one faces me, laughing at something the other in a short-sleeved button-down said. I know that laugh, that grin, that face.

Kevin Summers.

My heart stutters while everything else freezes. I can't remember the color of Rick's eyes, or if I even looked, but I remember Kevin's: that shade of green you only see right before a storm.

He's broader in the shoulders and more muscular now—he's grown into his stocky build. His hair is shorter than I recall; his well-groomed, wavy locks are now cut close to his head like a man in the military. That's it—that's what's different—Kevin looks like a man now. Still, he wears that expression like he's listening with his whole face.

The shorter, leaner, blond guy across from him reaches for Kevin's hand and doesn't let go. They're mid-conversation, casual, and comfortable. They're close—close enough to matter.

Seeing him hits like a sudden riptide beneath still water. I don't move—I can't. My mouth goes dry. My fingers curl against the denim in my pockets. Kevin looks happy. Settled. The other guy leans in to say something, and Kevin touches his wrist in response. It's a touch of familiarity—of intimacy.

It feels surreal, but it *is* him. He's right there and not alone.

I step backward into the awning's shadow and instinctively turn before he sees me. For a second, I consider walking over and saying his name, explaining what happened four years ago that night. But I'm not ready—not like this.

I don't look back until I've turned the corner, my heart still hammering. The air feels heavier, and I'm two blocks away before realizing I never got my coffee. It doesn't matter. My heart is beating too fast anyway. The last time I ran from Kevin, he was naked, and I was twenty.

Kevin is in Atlanta, and he's not alone.

I haven't seen him in four years, but one look—and everything I've buried comes rushing back.

I tell myself it's nothing. Just surprise. Just curiosity.

So why does it feel like the beginning of something I can't undo?

2

TWO TRUTHS AND A LIE

When I reach my apartment door, it feels like I've just dodged a meltdown. The hallway reeks of reheated Chinese and lemon-scented floor cleaner—the superintendent's lazy way of pretending age and mildew aren't slowly winning. Still, it's a great Craftsman-style brick building on 6th Street: three floors, each with four corner apartments and large factory windows framed by shaded oaks. Timing is everything. I was lucky when I found this place almost twelve months ago—and again this morning, slipping away from the café unseen.

I'm halfway to unlocking 2B when Naomi's voice cuts my focus. "Well damn, look what the nightlife spat out."

I turn, and she's leaning against her doorframe, 3C, arms crossed, one brow raised, that half-smirk pulling at her mouth like she's already read the ending of a chapter not written yet.

"Shit, you burn hotter than the skillet you just threw me on," I reply. Naomi is sharp-tongued, intelligent, unbothered, and lethal with one-liners.

"Well, if you weren't crawling in here like regret in a T-shirt, fresh off the walk of shame on a Sunday morning."

Naomi doesn't miss a thing. She's got eyes that can sniff out guilt before you're convicted. Late twenties, deep brown skin, shoulder-length braids, and a laugh you hear through walls. The first person I met in Atlanta and still my best friend—a freelance writer and editor by trade and full-time bullshit detector by birthright.

"You got someone in there still?" she asks, angling her head toward my half-open door.

I step in and nudge it shut with my foot. "No. He left."

Naomi checks her watch with a theatrical sigh, meaning she's about to deliver another line. "And it's not even noon. That's a record for you?"

"I need to shower and clean up," I say, closing the door and turning the lock like it might shut out more than neighbors.

"Uh-huh. Well, get your tragic ass cleaned up and dressed," Naomi shouts through the wooden door. "We're getting lunch at two o'clock. The usual spot."

The usual spot is a diner over on Myrtle, where Mateo works in the mornings. Naomi likes the corner booth. I like that no one asks how your night went unless you're bleeding.

"I'll meet you there," I shout back. "Let me rinse off the evidence of my poor decisions."

She chuckles, deep and sharp. "I'll bring holy water. In case you miss a spot."

~

By the time I walk in, Naomi is already sitting at the one table that doesn't wobble. She's mid-rant about a manuscript she's editing—some sad suburban memoir full of "we almost divorced, but then

7

we bought a boat" nonsense. Her iced tea sweats on the table beside a page full of underlined sentences and passive-aggressive edits.

Mateo walks over just as his shift ends, pulling his apron off like he's shedding a costume.

"Y'all don't wait for nobody, huh?"

Mateo Cruz has the kind of body you get from working two jobs and skipping the gym—solid, average, nothing flashy. Still, he wears it like he doesn't owe anyone an apology. He's got a bartender's smirk that never bothers to become a smile and eyes that track people like he's figuring out where they're most likely to tilt.

Mateo and I hooked up once, but it didn't work—too much deflection on my end and too much honesty on his, perhaps. We're better like this: part friends, mirror, and commentary.

"Sit down, pretty boy," Naomi says to Mateo, sipping her tea. "Danny here is about to confess something."

My stomach drops when she says this. For a split second, I think she knows. Somehow, through walls or instinct or whatever sixth sense Naomi walks around with, she saw me freeze on that sidewalk or spotted me duck into the café's shadow like a coward. She knows who Kevin is and that he's in Atlanta now. Naomi knows I saw him and that I am not okay.

But then I catch the direction of her comment, toward my apartment door and Rick's exit. She means him—last night's mistake, not this morning's surprise.

The panic drains as fast as it came, leaving something colder behind. Guilt, maybe. Relief's ugly twin.

"I'm not confessing anything," I say, wiping the condensation ring from her glass off the table with my napkin.

Naomi lifts her cup like she's toasting a lie. "Mm-hmm. You walked in like someone just pulled your file from the archives."

Mateo leans in, chin in hand. "This is about a guy?"

"What guy?" I ask too fast.

"See?" Naomi says. "There it is."

I could keep dodging. Make a joke. Pretend it's about Rick and call it a day. But the lie's already in my throat, half-swallowed and sour. What's the point of having friends if I keep spinning stories for an audience that already sees through the curtain?

Besides, saying it out loud might make it real. And real might be what I want.

A sigh escapes as I stare into my water like it might tell me what I'm actually feeling. "Fine," I say quietly. "I saw someone today. From before."

"From Bayview?" Mateo asks.

I nod once.

"Old boyfriend?" Naomi prods.

"Old... friend," I say, knowing it's not entirely true—not in the way they're hearing it.

Naomi tilts her head. "Uh-huh. One of those 'friends' you don't mention that creep outta your apartment in the middle of the night with their dignity half-buttoned? Like the one this morning?"

Naomi's not wrong. I glance up. "No," I reply.

Mateo arches a brow. "So? What'd he say?"

9

"I didn't talk to him."

Naomi's eyebrows lift. "You mean to tell me you had a trick last night, showed him out, and then 'ran into' another 'friend' and screwed him, too? Cause boy, I'mma gonna tell you, I heard you two banging last night. That was no 'old friend.' Sounded like somebody you left your mark on."

"You saw a friend from Bayview but didn't say anything to him? Why not?" Mateo asks, staying focused.

"He was with someone."

"Someone serious?" Mateo asks casually as if the answer doesn't matter. "Like a date serious, or like a boyfriend serious?"

"They looked… close," I answer.

Naomi leans in again. "So what's the problem if he's just an old friend from Bayview? Why didn't you say hi to him?"

"It's… complicated," I say, not fully understanding why I didn't say hi.

"Was this the guy in Bayview you told me about, right?" Mateo asks.

The nod comes before I can stop it, like I've seen a ghost— only it's the ghost of bad decisions past.

Mateo and Naomi exchange glances before she asks, "So, how did it feel to see him?"

I try to be neutral. "Strange. Familiar. Like a scene from a dream I forgot I had."

Naomi's voice stays gentle, but there's a knowingness in it. "Dreams don't walk into diners with boyfriends unless the universe is stirring your pot on purpose."

Mateo shakes his head. "You sure it's not just nostalgia? Sometimes, we rewrite what hurt into something that almost worked."

I don't answer. They didn't know what happened.

Naomi taps her nails against her glass. "You can't live in the past, chasing who you used to be."

I exhale slowly. "It's not that serious. I'm just curious."

She gives me a look like she's seen too many people mistake the match for the fire. "That's what folks say right before they burn the whole damn house down."

Mateo studies me. "So, you're going to try to track him down?"

I shrug. "I haven't decided."

That's a lie. My heart made up its mind the moment I saw Kevin—it's my courage that hasn't caught up. I tell myself I haven't decided, but the truth is quieter than that—more patient. It waits in the places I don't look: in the silence, in the water, in the spaces I keep trying to clean. I can lie to Naomi. I can even lie to myself. But eventually, the part of me that still remembers how it felt with Kevin will find a way to surface.

3

REFLECTIONS

The sun is already burning when I slip through the side gate into the backyard. It's the kind of place that could be on a magazine cover—hedges clipped into unnatural obedience, rows of white hydrangeas perfectly spaced as they bloom on command. The pool water glistens in the sunlight, still and pristine, framed by a stone deck that probably cost more than the house I grew up in.

My uniform shirt's already damp—light blue, logoed, with "Sunbelt Pool & Spa" stitched across the chest. When I set my equipment bag down, I peel the shirt off. The heat's a good excuse. Nobody questions it when you're sweating, even if it breaks company policy, but I do it anyway. Mr. and Mrs. Phillips wouldn't mind. They're cool people, especially considering their wealth, and both travel during the week for business. Still, they like the place to look perfect, even when they're not here. Me, a housekeeper, a lawn maintenance crew, a private gardener—all here twice weekly to fulfill the Phillips' needs.

The water calls to me—not spiritually, just instinctively. Familiar. It reminds me of a time not so long ago, when I was in high school and competing on the swim and dive team. It wasn't the competition that was appealing, but rather the freedom—the quiet isolation under the water's surface. It's the best part of the job, and why I took it. It's part of Bayview that I miss the most—

being surrounded by water: the lakes, the Bay, the Gulf, and the large pools with swim lanes at school. I miss the silence, the rhythm, the way it gives me something to do with my hands while my brain calms. Back then, it felt like I was moving toward something. These days, I'm just trying not to sink.

Dropping the vacuum hose into the deep end, I kneel to connect the line to the skimmer. The water ripples around the hose as it disappears beneath the surface—clean, blue, undisturbed. It reminds me of that night. Not all of the night, only flashes of it. The wet hush between words. The way I floated on my back while Kevin watched me. The way we belonged to the water—his bent knees under the surface supporting me when I sat on them—the stillness before everything changed.

I shake it off, shift my weight, and brush the walls of the pool. Focus. One tile at a time. The grout along the shallow end continues to collect more grime. Like everything else in life, it's the corners where things build up. But the flashes of that night keep coming anyway, uninvited.

His breath on my neck in the dark.

That pause before he asks if I've ever thought about being with another guy.

The flutter in my chest.

Finally, my answer. Yeah, I had wondered.

The way the pool's submerged light had glowed beneath us, casting luminous shapes on our legs, swimsuits, and torsos—the space between us pulsing with unfamiliar energy and warmth.

Focus, I remind myself again. I skim the surface first—leaves, a couple of dead insects, and a floating clear plastic straw wrapper blown in from another property. The water eventually captures everything discarded by nature and people alike.

The pole slides through the water as if it remembers every move I make before I make it. My body knows this. Like muscle memory. Like diving. Like Bayview.

Like him. Kevin.

I try to keep the name out, but it creeps in anyway. Soft at first. Just his voice. His laugh. The way he leaned in to touch the other guy's wrist. The window, the light behind him, the curve of his mouth when he smiled at someone who wasn't me.

I scrub the pool tiles harder than necessary.

Naomi's voice elbows into my memory: *Dreams don't walk into diners with boyfriends unless the universe is stirring your pot on purpose.*

I still don't know if spotting him was a dream or a warning.

I move to the filter basket and pull it up, shaking out anything skimmed off the surface. The pool is out in the open, so there's usually nothing. Every part of me tries not to go there, but my mind keeps skipping, like a scratched record, back to the one night I try to forget but have never been able to.

The pool's deck was wet. Kevin's bare skin glowed under the moonlight. I remember the sharp inhale when I touched his chest for the first time, unsure if I was allowed. The water was dark around us, warm from the day, cool against our skin. We stood in place, inches apart, the quiet so deep we could hear each other's heartbeat.

"Hey," a voice cuts through the haze of my remembrances.

I look up. The kid stands in the open doorway, silhouetted against the house behind him. He's shirtless, lean, and tanned. A towel is wrapped low around his hips, flip-flops smacking against the concrete as he walks out like he owns the sun.

"Didn't know you were coming today," he says, lowering his

head as he walks by, his Ray-Bans slipping just enough to peer over. His eyes are a sharp, oceanic blue, made even more striking by the blond hair that falls across his face like sunlit sand.

I nod. "Tuesdays and Fridays."

He sits and stretches on one of the loungers, settling in like he's done it a thousand times. His body is nothing special—not muscular or athletic—just young, tender, careless. The kind of body that has never been told no and hasn't yet learned what the word means. He watches me work, arms resting above his head, pretending not to watch me behind those dark, expensive sunglasses. Is he unaware of the ache he stirs? No, I think not.

I focus on the hose, lowering it into the water and letting it fill, air bubbling up in lazy bursts. I'm not tempted. Not really. But I know the feeling. The flicker. The way these setups begin.

His name is Patrick. I heard Mrs. Phillips say it once when I came by early and caught her on the phone arguing with him about a dent in the car, his grades, and an overdrawn expense account—standard rich people stuff. He's probably nineteen, a freshman at Vanderbilt. Not old enough to be appreciative, yet old enough to play games.

I glance up from my stare that has lasted too long. Patrick smirks.

Back to work.

I push and pull on the pole as the vacuum glides along the bottom, tracing the same lines repeatedly like I'm trying to remember something I told myself to forget.

Sometimes, my mind drifts to how much happened between Kevin and me that night. I think about what didn't—how close we got before it started to mean something.

Before I ran.

I wonder what I'd say if I saw him again. Not across a café with his hand in someone else's. I picture us bumping into each other at a bookstore or a bar. A moment of awkward surprise. I say, "Hey, long time." He says, "Daniel?" as if he's unsure whether it's a good or a bad thing to see me. If he's happy or not to see me. Maybe we talk, or perhaps we don't. Maybe he looks at me like I'm someone he used to know, and that's it.

Maybe that's all I deserve.

The kid stands and stretches again, a long and posed stretch, before walking toward the house like it's his turn. I feel his eyes on me before the door closes behind him.

Temptation's just a pattern I need to learn how to outwait.

I wrap the vacuum hose, rinse the deck, and pack my gear. I don't say it out loud, not even to myself—but the decision's already there, settled beneath the noise of everything else. It's the way Kevin's name keeps echoing, soft but constant. I tell myself it's just a thought, a memory. But thoughts don't linger like this. And memories don't look back at you across a café window. Not unless they want something. Not unless you do, too.

4

The Empty Seat

The smoke reaches me before Mateo does. It drifts through the warm evening air like a slow yearning, curling above the bamboo railing that separates the patio from the sidewalk. Naomi waves it away with a look that says she's tired of holding her tongue.

"You really have to do that before dinner?" she mutters.

Mateo steps back onto the patio and drops into his seat like he's settling into a couch. "It's not dinner. It's Thai tapas."

Naomi doesn't answer. She just gives him that side-eye squint she's perfected—equal parts disdain and affection—and stabs a piece of tofu with her fork.

I push my noodles around with chopsticks I never learned to use correctly. They're going cold.

"Okay," Naomi says, resting her elbow on the table. "You've been quiet for three minutes straight. That's never good."

Shrug. "Just tired. Hot as hell today."

"Yeah?" Mateo says, reaching for his water. "You sure it's not a different kind of heat?"

Naomi sighs. "Oh no."

He raises an eyebrow at me. "You were thinking about him

again, weren't you?"

Naomi sets her fork down with a little too much force. "Y'all are doing this right now?"

I don't look at either of them. "I wasn't going to bring it up."

"But you did," Mateo says.

I shift in my seat. The string lights above cast a warm haze over the table, softening the edges of everything except the knot tightening in my chest. I exhale slowly, then say it.

"I think I want to talk to him."

Naomi goes still.

Mateo blinks. "Wait. Kevin?"

I nod.

Naomi leans back in her chair, arms folded. "Why?"

"I don't know. It's just—seeing him that morning—I can't stop thinking about it."

Mateo whistles low. "One sighting and you're already planning the sequel?"

"It wasn't even a conversation. He didn't see me. But I haven't stopped thinking about it since."

Naomi tilts her head, studying me like I'm a puzzle that rearranged itself overnight. "And you think talking to him is a good idea?"

"I think it's just one conversation. Nothing more—"

Naomi cuts in before I can finish. "That's a lie, and you know it."

Her voice is sharper now, and Mateo's already poking the fire.

"I mean, what's the worst that happens?" Mateo says. "Kevin punches him? Cries? Confesses eternal love in the middle of Piedmont Park?"

Naomi groans. "Don't be stupid."

They go back and forth, voices rising and curling like the steam off our plates.

And I'm gone. Just like that, I'm thirteen again.

~

Sitting at the far end of the middle school lunch table, I rest one arm across my tray like a shield. It's January, one of those rare bone-cold days in Florida where no one wants to go outside, and the cafeteria smells like boiled green beans and bleach.

I keep my eyes on the clock above the vending machines.

Sixteen minutes until the bell. Sixteen minutes of pretending I don't hear the boys at the other table snickering or see how they look at my jeans—probably too tight, the length too high-water, the style too outdated.

Sixteen minutes of swallowing everything I wish I could say because saying it would make it real.

Across from me, there's an empty seat.

There's always an empty seat.

Some days, I pretend someone's about to fill it. Some friend who gets me—a version of me that's less shy, talks louder, laughs easier, and knows how to want something without choking on it.

I never give him a name. That would make it harder to admit

he's not coming. Maybe he was never coming. Or perhaps he has already found someone else to sit with.

The boys at the other table burst into laughter. One slams a milk carton until it explodes, but the teachers either don't notice or, if they do, choose not to.

I stare at the empty seat until the bell rings.

~

"Daniel?"

Naomi's voice pulls me back in, and I blink.

Mateo is smirking over his curry. Naomi's leaning in again, watching me.

I clear my throat and reach for my water. "Sorry. Zoned out for a second. What were you saying?"

Naomi raises an eyebrow. "I said, you're lying to yourself if you think talking to him is a good idea. That you can pick right back up where you left off."

"That's not what I'm doing," I say. "Kevin looked different. Like he's moved on. And I have, too. I just—"

"Need closure?" Naomi cuts in. "Because baby, that's the oldest excuse in the book."

Mateo, still watching me, says quietly, "What would you even say?"

The glass sweats quietly between my hands, condensation pooling underneath. "Maybe..." I pause. "Well, I'm not sure."

Naomi's voice lowers. "You're not looking for answers. You're chasing the version of you that disappeared the night you ran. And guess what? That Daniel? He's gone."

I don't say anything. Because I don't know what to say. Naomi's not wrong.

But she's not right either.

Mateo breaks the silence with a smile that's almost kind. "Okay, but what if this version of Kevin has a boyfriend and a mortgage now?"

"Then I'll say hi and go home."

Naomi rolls her eyes. "Bullshit."

We let the quiet hang for a minute. Someone at another table laughs. A car honks its horn a block away. The scent of grilled scallions fills the air.

Mateo stands and pulls out another cigarette. Naomi watches him, incredulous. "Can you not for five minutes?"

He winks at her, then steps away toward the sidewalk.

As they bicker, a napkin drifts toward me on the breeze, and I catch it. Naomi says something about lung cancer and needing new friends. I click the pen left by the waitress and quietly write his name: *Kevin Summers. Atlanta.*

Naomi and Mateo walk ahead, still bickering—she about toxins, he not listening. I hang back under the string lights, their voices fading as I slip the napkin into my pocket like a promise I'm not ready to keep.

In front of me is the past. Somewhere up the block is the future. And in between? Still me—still waiting for someone to fill the empty seat. I follow slowly, unsure if I'm moving toward something real or just running from the quiet again. Maybe I'll go home. Perhaps I won't. But I already know I won't sleep.

5

THE WRONG KIND OF WARMTH

The Anvil smells like sweat, beer, and leather. It feels humid and wrong the second I step inside. Just past the door, hands still buried in my pockets, the urge to leave hits almost immediately. I've never been here before, so I tell myself it's just for a quick drink. I'm just here to see what the place is like. I'm just here to remind myself I can still disappear into something or someone if I need to.

The lights are dim, and the air is thick. It's a place where no one sees you; they just scan you. I slowly move through the club, taking it all in and brushing past men who don't look twice or for too long. There's a bar and a dance floor, complete with a DJ booth and a metal cage hanging from the ceiling. Past it, a leather shop stocked with oils, harnesses, and other gear. In the back, the hallway of shame leads to the darkroom. Someone whistles from the shadows as I pass, but I don't stop.

I won't run into Kevin in a place like this, but I knew that before I walked in.

The bar is sticky under my elbow. I order a vodka tonic with lime and take a sip before slamming the whole thing back. It's like watching myself from a few feet away—tired, out of place, pretending to be okay. Pretending this is me, and I'm fine being here.

I feel him before I see him. Brawny. Confident. Maybe thirty-five. I'm six-one, and he's at least an inch taller than I am. He moves like he's done this before, like he knows the room is watching him with anticipation, and he's meeting their expectations. His shirt is tight across his chest, sleeves rolled up, like a lumberjack; the sweat on his chest hair catches the glow of one of the few pin lights in the room. He looks straight at me when he approaches.

"You new here?" he asks, already too close. Too assertive.

"Not really," I say in an octave lower than usual, trying to sound as solid as he looks, to square my shoulders with my voice.

He smirks like I had already said yes. "You've got that look."

"What look?"

"Like you've been too good for too long, so now you're here."

I glance down at my drink, then back up. I don't answer, and I don't smile. But I don't walk away either. That's the part that bothers me.

The lumberjack's hand finds the small of my back as if he owns it. My first reaction is to stiffen, which I do for a second, but then I relax. Maybe this is why I came here. If I can't be satisfied, perhaps I can at least be wanted.

"Want to go back?" he says, tipping his head toward the red-lit hallway.

I hesitate. It's barely a second, but I feel it in my stomach. Then I nod.

The back room is even darker than I imagined. Bodies shift through shadows. I hear heavy breathing and grunting. Someone whispers in the far corner, and it sounds like a dare.

The lumberjack leads me into a half-lit alcove where a bench lines the wall. There's no door, just shadows, breathing, and the faint, wet sounds of other bodies deeper in the darkness. No one stops us. No one looks.

His hand lands on my shoulder, large and heavy, guiding me down like we've done this before. I sit on the bench, and he looms over me.

It's fast from there. Too fast.

Yet, I still let it happen. Because walking out would mean going home and sitting alone, feeling everything. I'm so fucking tired of feeling everything and feeling nothing at the same time.

For a second, I let myself believe that letting someone else take over might be a relief—that maybe if he calls the shots, I won't have to want or feel. I won't have to think about Kevin, hate myself, or relive that night again. Yet, I don't want to forget it either.

I used to be good at this—this pretending—this disappearing into someone else's heat. I told myself it was freedom, that it made me brave. Now, it just makes me cold.

The lumberjack lifts me off the bench in one swift motion, gripping my chest and driving me back into the wall. His weight presses in. His mouth finds mine—rough, urgent, without tenderness. I allow it on autopilot, but I'm not here—not really.

Then his hands are at my waist, pulling at my belt like he owns it—hurried, rough, trying to turn me toward the wall with an urgency that surprises me.

"Slow down," I growl, my breathing exasperated, but I'm not sure he hears me—or cares.

He pulls back just enough to look at me. There's a grin, but it's the wrong kind. "Damn," he says. "You're one of those pretty boys who likes to play shy."

His hand clamps on my jaw, tilting my face with a force that makes me freeze, like I'm something he thinks owes him.

"But I know what you want," he snarls back, pressing his mouth to mine—hard, forceful, like a command I never gave. His hands are everywhere. On my belt. My chest. My neck.

And something inside me snaps.

He doesn't know me. He doesn't see me. I let him get this close, hoping to feel something, but all I feel is anger.

"No!" I shout.

He doesn't move. Just smirks. "Relax."

I shove him hard, using the wall behind me as leverage with one foot.

"What the fuck?" he spits, more annoyed than hurt. He looks confused but not afraid. Like I've broken the rules.

I stand fast, my body suddenly coiled, my heart slamming in my chest. "Back off, asshole!"

He straightens up, all attitude. "Jesus. It's a queer bar, not a fucking church."

But I don't wait. I push past the asshole and out into the hall, my breath ragged, hands shaking. My face is hot like it's burning from the inside. I feel watched. Judged. Followed. I don't look back.

Pushing through the crowd shoulder-first, I ignore whoever calls after me. I'm outside before I realize I'm running.

The night air hits me like punishment, cold against my sweat-damp skin, and I gulp it like water. My hands won't stop shaking. My feet pound the sidewalk before I can tell them where to go. My shirt is half-buttoned, and my pulse won't slow down.

I feel stupid. I feel dirty. I feel like I said yes to the wrong thing to avoid the right one.

How did I let that happen?

How the hell could I have thought that would help?

The walk home is a blur. I keep walking, one foot in front of the other. No music. No cab. Only the sound of my shoes hitting the pavement and the burn in my throat every time I try to swallow.

By the time I reach my apartment, the keys are slick in my hand, and I fumble with the lock like I've forgotten how doors work. When it finally clicks open, I step inside and shut it hard behind me. The slam echoes, and I wait in the silence, just breathing.

No one followed me. No one cared enough to.

I can't go on like this.

Stripping in the hallway without turning on the lights, I toss my clothes into the hamper without looking at them. I don't want to see myself right now. I don't want to catch my reflection and have to explain what the hell I thought I was doing.

As I stand there naked, steam rises from the shower as the water heats. I step in and crank it as hot as I can take—until my skin stings and the mirror fogs over. The water hits me like a slap, and I let it. I deserve it.

I scrub harder than necessary, chasing some illusion of control I can't reach. My skin prickles under the heat. I scrub like I can scrape off the night. Like I can erase myself.

My jaw aches where he grabbed it. I close my eyes and see him again—his smirk, his grip, the way he said 'pretty boy' like it was both a compliment and a warning.

I thought I could handle it. I thought I wanted it. But what I really wanted was to feel something other than alone. I shut the water off when it finally runs cold, but the silence is worse than the heat.

I towel off without completely drying, drop the towel on the floor, and walk to the bedroom. I lie on the bed, damp and hollow, arms folded over my chest like armor. Beads of water drip from my hair into the pillow as I stare at the ceiling.

The room feels unfamiliar. I feel unfamiliar. This person isn't who I want to be. But it's who I am tonight—still chasing the wrong kind of warmth.

This wasn't about sex. Not really. That, at least, I understand. It was about not feeling alone, yet now I'm lonelier than ever.

I don't know what hurts more—the fear, or how close I came to calling it comfort.

6

CHANCE ENCOUNTER

The plastic grocery bag digs into my palm. It's not heavy—just a sandwich, some chips, and a bottle of tea I'm not even thirsty for—yet I shift it again anyway. I've got two pools left today and plenty of time to make it to them, but I'm still lingering outside Publix like I'm waiting for something.

Maybe I am. Or perhaps I'm just avoiding something.

A warm breeze stirs the air as I lean on the fountain's ledge in the center of Ansley Mall's open courtyard. It carries the scent of sun-warmed concrete, cigarette smoke, and espresso wafting from the Starbucks patio beside the bookstore. People flow past me: gym rats, lunch-hour office types, retirees power-walking with fanny packs and mirrored sunglasses.

The world is busy, distracted, and normal. Most of the world, anyway.

It's been two days since The Anvil. Two days since I let myself be cornered and handled like a body with no name. Since I shoved a stranger off me in the dark and ran through the doors like I'd just escaped a fire.

I haven't told Mateo or Naomi yet. I haven't said the words out loud: I searched for touch and found a threat. I keep replaying it in flashes—the hand at my jaw, the smirk, the way he said 'pretty boy' like I should be flattered.

I think of Mr. and Mrs. Phillips' son, Patrick, the boy by the pool—quiet, watchful, all soft edges and stillness. Maybe there had been want in his eyes, but it didn't come with danger. He didn't push—just waited, quiet and unsure, like he needed permission. I don't know. Maybe it was just the moment I was in—or perhaps I'm just projecting.

But here I am, still sweating, eating my lunch alone in the middle of a busy courtyard, thinking about ghosts whose meanings I haven't even named out loud: the lumberjack, the rich college student, one-night-stand Jack, and the old friend with his affectionate blond. Naomi said to leave it alone. Mateo said to recheck the café. But right now, none of it feels like a plan—just a stalling tactic.

I pick up my tea and toss the sandwich wrapper, satisfied for now, as I head back toward the lot and the two jobs left for the day.

And there he is, right in front of me, walking out of the gym doors as they swing open.

Kevin.

Stepping into the sunlight from Fitness Factory, like the universe read my thoughts and gave me what my heart wasn't ready for, because my mind couldn't decide.

He's tanned and relaxed. A gym bag slung over his shoulder, hair still damp, dressed in black slacks and an indigo-blue button-down. Polished shoes, casual posture—like someone used to looking sharp without trying. He looked different at the café—more casual. Today, he's polished. Controlled.

I lock up as he pauses just beyond the door like he's recalibrating—scanning the sidewalk. He spots me almost immediately.

Our eyes meet, and it's too late to look away, unlike I did on Sunday at the café. He's seen me, lifting one hand in an easy wave—a friendly acknowledgment—walking toward me.

My breath catches. I feel everything in my chest collapse and expand at once. *Shit*, I think to myself. I'm wearing my pool company's polo and have spent half the day working out in the sun. I just ate lunch and likely have food between my teeth. *Fuck!*

"Daniel? Hey buddy!" His voice is easy and familiar, as if this is normal, like I didn't vanish almost four years ago and take something with me.

"Hey," I manage.

Kevin walks over slowly, neither hesitating nor rushing. He leaves just enough space between us, close enough to talk but not close enough to be intimate.

"Didn't expect to run into you here," he says, adjusting the strap of his gym bag.

"Yeah," I say, lifting the tea. "Just grabbing lunch." His gaze drops to it and back again. He smiles just enough to show that familiar indent near his cheek.

"You working nearby?"

"Sort of. Midtown and Buckhead today. Pool maintenance," I say, pointing to the logo on my shirt.

He nods at what I tell him, like that makes perfect sense. "You look good."

I swallow. "Thanks," I say. "So do you. Working out, I see."

Kevin's eyes flick to the coffee shop across the courtyard, then around us as if to ensure no one is watching. His smile changes— less polite, more uncertain.

"I thought that was you outside of Corner Café on Sunday."

My stomach drops.

"You saw me?" I ask.

He shrugs, suddenly shy. "At first, I wasn't sure, but I guess it was."

"And you didn't...?"

"I didn't know if I should."

I nod like I understand. But I don't. Not really. I'm too busy feeling the blood rush to my ears.

He looks down, then back at me. "I'm not saying I should've ignored you. I was just surprised, I guess."

"Yeah," I say. Saying anything else feels too much.

There's movement all around us—cars pulling into angled spaces, a woman unlocking her bike from the rack behind me, and two friends hugging goodbye as they split off toward different shops. The publicness of it feels raw—this casual exposure, this moment in plain sight. The fact that anyone could walk by and see this—see me—talking to Kevin and not know that it feels like time just doubled back on itself.

More footsteps. A car horn blares. A group of guys exits the gym behind Kevin, laughing loudly, and he instinctively steps half a pace closer to me, like trying to carve out a space where we can still be alone. But he doesn't stay there long.

"I should get going," he says finally. "I'm already running late."

I nod. "Yeah, me too."

He hesitates, then asks, "You have a number?"

I shake my head before I even think. "No, not yet."

His face registers something—not quite disappointment or surprise—just recalculation.

"Uhm," he says lightly as he thinks, and I hear what he's not saying.

"You could give me your work number," I offer. "I'll call sometime."

He glances over his shoulder, pulls a folded receipt from his bag, and scribbles a number in thick blue ink.

"Office," he says. "It's a direct line."

I take the paper. Our hands don't touch, but my skin warms like they did. The receipt goes into my back pocket before I can let myself look.

"Cool," I say. "Thanks."

He smiles once more—guarded but real. "Talk soon?"

"Yeah. Definitely."

And then he walks off, gym bag bouncing at his hip, blending back into the world that doesn't know what just shifted.

I stand there momentarily, letting the noise return to normal, allowing the ache to settle into something quieter. I touch the receipt in my back pocket, still feeling the phantom heat of his hand.

I no longer get to pretend or wonder. Kevin's here. He saw me. All this time, I thought I'd be the one to choose if—or when—we spoke again. But he beat me to it. Now, the silence is mine to break. The only choice left is whether I call or disappear again.

7

The Edge of Yes

The apartment is quiet, like the stillness of hesitation, but my mind isn't. I've stripped my work polo, showered off the smell of chlorine and sun, and thrown on a clean tee and boxers. The day's heat lingers—not just on my skin, but deep inside, tight and unsettled. The air conditioner hums in the corner, pushing the cool air. On the counter, the receipt with Kevin's number lies flat and smoothed out, damp from where it sat in my back pocket all afternoon.

Kevin saw me. He saw me outside the café last Sunday and said nothing, but today, he did. He walked right up and said hello as if it were nothing, like it hadn't been four years since everything flipped upside down and never got put back.

I should feel relieved, satisfied, or maybe validated. But what I feel is off guard, like I've been stripped of the choice and called out on a bluff I didn't realize I was making.

I keep walking past it.

The toast from breakfast is stale, and I'm still full from lunch, but I nibble at it anyway. I stare at the half-dead pothos plant on the shelf, turning the radio dial until I land on something low and melancholy—instrumental jazz. It fills the space but doesn't change it. The room still feels like it's watching me.

I consider calling and think about what I'd say and what I

wouldn't.

Kevin had said, "Talk soon?"

And I had replied, "Definitely."

Then I walk to the window and look through the oak branches and leaves at the cars parked along the curb. There's not much to see, only someone walking their dog in a ratty T-shirt and pajama pants. The city never really goes quiet; it slightly softens.

And suddenly, it comes back, like a flicker in my periphery, like a memory tapping me on the shoulder.

He used to say life's full of tiny detours. The gas station you don't mean to stop at. The old friends you didn't expect to run into. And I'm there again. Back before I ruined it.

~

(Four Years Earlier)

I'm not even sure why I'm here. The fight wasn't new—same old shouting and silence after. Stacy slammed the door behind her, and I grabbed my keys like I had somewhere to be. The truth is, I only needed space and air.

I'm standing in the fluorescent glow of a convenience store, walking between shelves of general merchandise—a whole grocery store condensed into one short aisle of overpriced basics. I don't need or want any of it. I'm not hungry. I'm drifting, killing time before going home to apologize for whatever she says I did or didn't do.

I sense movement in the next aisle—someone's shoulder, the rustle of chip bags, the weight of a gaze. Then I hear it.

"Daniel?"

I freeze. It's been a couple of years, maybe more, but I'd know that voice anywhere. I look up and see Kevin standing at the end of the aisle, eyes wide, a small smile breaking across his face like he's unsure if this is real.

"I don't believe it," he says.

"Hey, bud," I manage, the words tumbling from my mouth like muscle memory.

He steps around the endcap, his hand out like it's high school again. He has the same clean look and the same posture, though slightly older and weary in the eyes. He pats my shoulder as we shake hands. I try to keep it casual.

"So, what's new?" he asks.

I shrug, hands deep in my pockets. "Not much. Same old stuff."

"You working? Not in school, right?"

"Hell no." I laugh, even though nothing's funny. "You know how much I loved school. I'm working for my dad again. Got married, too."

Kevin blinks. "No shit. Married to who?"

"You remember Stacy? We got married last year. Got a place a few blocks away." I don't mention that it's only a rental, an old single-wide in a trailer park that smells like mildew and burnt coffee. I don't mention the part where I sleep on the couch half the time.

Kevin nods like he remembers, even though I can tell he

doesn't. It doesn't matter.

"Well, congratulations," he says, but something in his face shifts—like he's doing math that doesn't quite add up.

"Thanks, man," I say, but my voice tightens. "She's a bitch, though. Big mistake. We fight all the fucking time. That's why I'm here. Needed a breather."

Kevin nods, slower this time. There's a flicker in his eyes—something like understanding or pity.

"Sorry," he says. I wait for more, but that's all he gives me.

Then Kevin says, "Hey, I was grabbing snacks for a movie with Alice. You remember her. My aunt."

"Yeah, sure," I say, smiling without meaning to. I remember her barging into Kevin's pool party when his parents went out of town on vacation, yelling at us to shut it down.

"She's cool," he echoes. "I'm staying with her right now. Want to come chill with us?"

I hesitate—one breath. I don't know what I'm walking into or what this is. But something about the way Kevin looks at me, the way his voice dips low, makes it inviting and easy to say, "Sure, why not? Got anything to drink? Want me to grab some cold brewskies, dude?"

"Yeah, sure, beer is cool," he says, and I can hear the eye roll in his voice. Still, he's smiling. That warmth is still there, buried under whatever weight he's carrying now.

We grab our things and head to the parking lot.

"It's just a few blocks away," he says, tossing his bag into the passenger seat.

"I'll follow," I say, slipping into my car. As I pull out behind him, I feel something shift in my chest. I don't know what tonight is, but it beats loitering at convenience stores, stuck in a toxic marriage, letting life happen to me, waiting for change without ever causing it, just becoming someone I never meant to be.

~

The ceiling fan clicks above me in the dark. I'm on my back in bed, the memory of that chance reuniting echoing through my brain like it just happened, like I'm still in that pool, suspended between choices I couldn't name.

He said it first. But I didn't stop him. And then I walked away.

That was the worst part.

I ran. I *always* run.

Now he's here. In this city. At that café. Stepping out of that gym with a smile and a number on a folded receipt sitting on the table beside me.

I grip the spare pillow and hold it close to my body, closing my eyes.

What I want is unclear. What I remember, though—that's vivid.

And I'm standing on the edge of yes—again—and still unsure if I'll jump.

8

SUNLIGHT AND SHADOWS

It's just past two when the Phillips' gate clicks shut behind me. The Friday sun blazes like it hasn't moved all day. The air smells of jasmine and temptation, sweet and heavy like summer holding its breath. The pool glistens—blue, glassy, still—framed by neatly clipped hedges and sun-bleached concrete. There's no radio playing, no distant lawn mower, no noise drifting over the fence. Just the hum of the filter and the far-off buzz of cicadas, their steady drone rising and falling like audible heat.

And then I see him. It's just like clockwork. A coincidence? I wonder.

He's stretched out in a lounge chair across the deck, lying on his stomach with one arm slung over his head and the other dangling limply off the side. Patrick is shirtless again, but this time wearing a light blue Speedo rather than the green swim trunks he wore last Tuesday. His headphones cover his ears, the cord trailing into a small cassette player resting on a towel near his hip. His back rises and falls with the rhythm of someone fully asleep or pretending to be.

I get to work uncoiling the vacuum hose, connecting the skimmer, and testing the chlorine. I check the filters and sweep the tiles—the usual tasks I perform each time I'm here—anything to stay busy. But my eyes keep drifting.

His skin is smooth and pale, with just the faintest tan line forming around his waistband. He will darken quickly if he continues his apparent tanning routine. His hair looks damp at the ends as if he had swum earlier and let the sun do the rest. The leg closest to me dangled over the lounger, the other stretched long, his calf tensed, like mid-dream. An unconscious pose, perhaps. Or not.

I catch myself staring too long and force my eyes back to the brush as I run along the pool's bottom.

I peel my shirt off, partly because of the heat, partly because I always do when skimming the deep end. My body's changed since Bayview. I've kept the lean swimmer's frame, but the daily work grind carved it harder—shoulders broader, lines sharper. Pool work keeps me cut without trying, and I know how I look now when I move.

Sometimes, in the mirrored sliding doors at homes like this, I catch my reflection without meaning to—angles and motion mid-stride—the slope of my obliques, the faint ridges above my hips. My chest is fuller than it used to be, and my muscles are more defined, rising and falling with each breath. I watch how the upper fibers flex when I push the pole forward, how my shoulders bunch and pull as I drag it back in long, steady strokes. The tendons shift visibly beneath the skin now—neck to collarbone to pec, a quiet sync of effort and control.

The reflection catches me straightening—maybe an unconscious pose, just in case he's watching. Of course, he's not. Or perhaps he is. It's hard to tell behind those sunglasses.

Thoughts of Kevin slip in—him stepping out of the gym, his eyes warm and familiar. Kevin, four years ago, with his sensitivity and seductiveness. Kevin, three days ago—the way he looked at me: not prowling, not possessive—just open, writing his number on a receipt for me. Maybe he'd been waiting, too, but then I remember the blond boy he was with at the café on Sunday, and I change my mind.

But now, in this heat and stillness, it's Patrick I see—all ease and silence. No demands. No expectations. Just skin, innocence, and the slow rise and fall of possibility.

And in my head, I imagine what could happen.

I picture walking over, slowly pulling off my shorts, and leaning above him. Maybe his eyes open, or they don't. I touch his back, just a brush of my fingertips, and he doesn't stop me. He wants it. He's been waiting for it.

In the fantasy, I'm confident. I'm in control. I straddle the chair, gently remove the headphones, and murmur something he barely hears before gently kissing his neck and exhaling warmth into his ear. I roll him over, and his mouth is soft, surprised at first, then eager. I trail my fingers down his sides and feel him harden under me. In this version, I'm the one taking, not asking. No flashbacks, no questions. Just movement, friction, escape.

But that's all it is: a fantasy, a flicker. Patrick is me four years ago, and I'm now Kevin: older, more experienced, more dangerous. I want to be Patrick, though, with Kevin above me, and then I hate myself for thinking it.

I plunge the net in hard and swirl it aggressively across the surface of the deep end, trying to shake the thought loose. Patrick's just a kid, nineteen or maybe twenty. But he appears younger, like someone who hasn't decided who he is yet and still has the chance to become someone he won't regret. I can't decide if that's what draws me to him or why I should leave him alone.

A splash of water from the skimmer hits the concrete and my legs, jolting me out of it.

Then I hear him.

"Mister Pool Guy," he says, his voice groggy and teasing. "You trying to splash me?"

I glance up. Patrick is sitting upright now, headphones around his neck, eyes squinting into the sun. There's a lazy grin tugging at his mouth.

"Sorry," I say, straightening.

"I didn't see you come in," he counters, stretching his arms over his head like a cat.

I look away too fast. "Didn't want to wake you."

"Well, too late now," he says, rubbing his chest like scratching an itch. "Are you always this quiet when you clean?"

"Depends on who's around," I say, immediately regretting the flirt in my tone.

Patrick catches it, though. He doesn't drop his gaze.

"Guess I'm lucky, then," he says.

Silence hovers between us. Not heavy—but charged.

I wipe my hands with the small towel around my belt loop, aware of how my face probably looks—flushed from the sun, still damp with sweat, eyes squinting against the glare.

I've got that look people tell me is intense when I'm not trying. Thick brows, deep-set eyes. The kind of face that always seems to be thinking, even when it's blank. Girls used to say it was sexy. Men in Atlanta say it's dangerous. Patrick hasn't said anything, but I can sense how he sees me—like I'm already halfway unwrapped.

"I should finish up," I say, returning toward the pool.

"Take your time," he says. "I like watching you work."

A glance over my shoulder confirms it. Patrick is reclined again, but he's sitting, facing me this time. His headphones are back in place, but he's not pressing play. He's just watching me, grinning—his legs spread, his knees at least shoulder-length apart, the way guys tend to sit when they're relaxed. I see his elbows resting on the arm of the lounger, his hands landing casually on his upper thighs, his fingers dangerously close to the elastic of the Speedo—its light blue hue leaving little to the imagination. Its material is barely able to contain the outline of his arousal.

I pack my equipment more slowly than I need to, then raise my shirt above my head before allowing it to slide over my torso, feeling his eyes on me the whole time. I want to take it off again: just to pose, to tempt, to provoke. But I don't. Not this time, anyway.

When I leave, I don't say goodbye. I don't need to. This isn't over yet.

9

SOMEWHERE ELSE

Naomi knocks on my door around six. Her voice is bright and casual. "Dinner? I'm thinking Colonnade. Real butter and big portions. You in?"

I haven't moved since I got home: still in my towel from the shower, still warm from the sun, sprawled across the bed like the day never ended.

"Rain check?" I yell.

Naomi doesn't press. She clicks her tongue and says, "You better eat something that isn't pickles and Triscuits. I'm serious."

"I will. Promise."

"Mmhm," I hear her say as she descends the stairs toward the front door. I hear no guilt, just enough neighborly love to sting.

Four hours later, I'm awake from a nap I hadn't intended to take. I throw on jeans and a tee and stride out into the dark.

~

Burkhart's is quieter than usual for a Friday night—at least upstairs, where Mateo tends bar at night. The lighting is low and golden, bouncing off the polished wood counter as if the whole place is sealed in amber glass. Synth-pop hums through the speakers—something danceable but subdued. I've been nursing a vodka tonic for twenty minutes before Mateo finally makes his way upstairs to take over.

"Didn't think I'd see you tonight," he says, sliding a rag across the bar as he stops in front of me. "Thought you and Naomi would be hanging out."

"She invited me," I say, taking a slow sip. "I passed."

Mateo raises an eyebrow. "Damn. You're spiraling."

"She wanted Colonnade, but I wasn't in the mood to be sociable tonight."

Mateo tosses the rag over his shoulder and leans on his elbows. "Alright. What is it then? Brooding? Longing dramatically at a half-empty glass?"

I manage a half-smile. "Just wanted a cocktail."

He studies me, then nods toward the drink. "Only one?"

"I don't know."

He reaches under the bar, pulls out a lime wedge, and plunks it onto a napkin in front of me. "You don't usually drink alone. You okay?"

I shrug, which means no.

Mateo folds his arms. "It's that guy, Kevin, right?"

"Kevin," I confirm.

"So, what, you still thinking about tracking him down?"

I shake my head. "No. I ran into him. We talked."

Mateo's face goes slack with surprise. "You talked?"

I nod. "Yesterday."

"And?"

"And nothing," I say. "He was nice. He gave me his number, but I haven't called."

Mateo taps his fingers against the wood. "You know I'm gonna ask the obvious."

"Why haven't I called?"

He nods.

"Because if I call, it's real. And I don't know which version of Kevin I'll get."

Mateo huffs. "That's your excuse? Not even curious? That's next-level cowardice, mi amigo."

My eyes narrow. "Thanks for the support."

"I'm just saying," he says, voice softening. "He saw you. You saw him. That's an opportunity, not a lifetime guarantee."

I don't answer. I down the last of my drink and let the ice settle.

Mateo tilts his head. "Look—maybe it's nothing. Maybe it's not what you think it is. But if it is, you've already done the hard part, right? You know how to reach him."

"Sure, except now I can't stop *seeing* him in my mind."

"Then call him, or don't," he says, pushing off the bar and turning to make another drink. "But pick a lane, buddy. This middle shit's gonna rot your gut."

He's already walking away before I can come up with a retort. And then it hits—that slow, familiar burn of someone watching me.

The bar's not crowded, but it has that growing Friday buzz—people unwinding from the week. Mateo pours two drafts, wipes his hands, and moves to the corner where I've planted myself. I sit on a wooden stool, elbows resting on the counter, staring past the liquor shelf to the mirror behind it.

"You always look like you're solving equations when you drink alone," he says.

"It's either this or pacing my apartment."

Mateo leans against the bar again, eyes scanning my face. "You gonna call him?"

"Maybe."

"That's something," Mateo says, shrugging. "Just saying—you looked different when you talked about him."

"Different, how?"

"Like you gave a shit. Like it wasn't just a passing thing."

I exhale through my nose, the only laugh I can manage. "I don't even know what it is."

"Doesn't have to be anything. It could be closure or something new. But you won't find out from this barstool."

I lift my glass and finish it in two gulps.

Mateo grins. "I'll get your next one. You look like you need a do-over."

While he pours, someone sits next to me. He's older, maybe in his late twenties—stocky, five o'clock shadow, smells like cologne and cigarettes.

"You always come in here looking that conflicted, or is tonight special?" he asks.

I glance sideways. "Just tired."

He leans back against the bar, eyeing me, then tilts his head as if he's unconvinced. "You don't look tired. You look like someone waiting to make a mistake."

He says it like a compliment. I let it hang there, waiting for the punchline that doesn't come.

He smiles and leans in slightly. "Let me guess. Someone did you dirty."

"Does it matter?"

"Nah," he says.

I can feel his gaze travel around the bar, then rest back on me. I don't look at him.

"You're not gonna find the answer in that glass," he adds.

"No," I say as I stand. "But maybe I'll find it somewhere else."

He chuckles as I stand. "If you change your mind," I hear him say as I walk away.

I find Mateo and thank him for the drink. "I'm heading home," I add. "And do me a favor. The asshole who sat next to me at the end of the bar—Visine his next drink for me."

Mateo tilts his head, giving me that slow, incredulous look from under his brows. "Call him, dumbass."

~

The radio's low as I head home, but I'm not listening. I drive— city lights flickering off the hood, traffic lights changing without urgency, the night humming low and indifferent. Mateo's voice still resounds in my head. So does Kevin's face. So does Patrick's.

I catch myself tapping the steering wheel as if trying to knock something loose. Mateo said to call him. Or not. Just pick a lane. The moment stretches, and the drive slows. I pass the turn for my street but keep going. I drive in wide circles on city streets around

Midtown. After twenty minutes, what began as a drift becomes a decision.

I could've gone home. I meant to. I even passed my turn. But the apartment felt too safe—too familiar for my mood—and I needed somewhere darker than memory.

I turn left, then swing a right down Cheshire Bridge Road, headed to a different kind of place—a different kind of quiet. I pass neon signs for adult video stores, closed diners, and a shuttered pawn shop with bars on the windows. The further I go, the more I disappear. It's not that I'm drawn to this place. It's that I don't want to be anywhere else.

The complex doesn't look like much—just rows of concrete block structures painted gray in a nondescript industrial park. There are other units just like it, to the left and right, but all are closed except for this one, which has an unlit sign above the door that reads "Steamworks." I park in the back of the building, near the black metal entrance door, and see a few men going in, their heads down, shoulders squared. I follow.

The man at the counter and glass window doesn't ask for ID; he asks for a membership card, purchased daily for five dollars and valid for twenty-four hours. He asks if I want to rent a room. I decline. He takes my cash and slides me a towel and a key with a locker number. I nod and push through the metal door to the locker area, stripping down like it's not my first time. It isn't. Mateo brought me here once, a few weeks after our first and only date, convinced we needed friendship more than we needed each other's sex. I don't know how often he frequents this place—we don't talk about it. I only know he's working tonight, so he won't see me here.

I shove my clothes into the locker, wrap the towel low around my hips, and step into the main corridor. The lighting is low and red-tinted, nearly swallowed by the black ceiling and dark walls lined with private rooms. The hallway smells like disinfectant and something sourer—like desperation scrubbed but not removed. Figures drift through the dim corridors like shadows. I don't want introductions. I want to forget.

There's a video room with sofas and a large projection screen at the end of the hallway. It's a place where guys drift in to rest or lose themselves in the flicker of looping adult films. Some just watch. Others linger along the wall. A few eventually join in, wordless and slow, as if following an unspoken script.

Beyond the video room, another hallway lined with partitions, some occupied by men turned inward, their bodies pressed to the barriers, seeking something faceless on the other side. It reminds me of a milking station at a dairy, and I tread past them. Perhaps I'll return.

This hallway leads to a steam room and a jacuzzi. Signs near the jacuzzi remind guests of health rules and discourage anything beyond relaxation. The steam room, by contrast, carries a different kind of expectation—one that goes unspoken but understood.

I weave through a series of short passageways—a labyrinth of turns—until I reach the final room: the darkroom. It's pitch black. I can't see my hand in front of my face, even when I bring it to my nose. But that's the point. The space isn't for sight. It's for what happens when vision is denied. I can't tell how large it is, how many others are inside, or what any of them look like—and that, too, seems intentional.

I inch my way into the dark, one small step at a time, hands outstretched to avoid bumping into anything or anyone. My fingers find a wall, and then, a shift in the air. A presence. The darkness smells thick and close, rank in a way that suggests too much human heat sealed in too small a space, like a towel used for something private and left unwashed. It clings.

I want to run, but instead, I keep moving, drawn forward by the soundscape around me. Kissing, muffled groans, the shuffle of bodies shifting in the dark. But louder than any of it is the pounding of my own heart in my ears. The air is thick and humid, laced with a musk that I can almost taste. It settles on my tongue like a warning.

Still, I shuffle my feet forward, relieved that I kept my sneakers on. Then the sense of touch takes over—but it's not mine. It's theirs. A hand on my back slides down to my waist, gripping with a pressure that makes me tense. Another grazes my stomach from behind, fingers tracing up and down my abs. I tighten them out of reflex—vanity, maybe. I don't know why I do it. It's automatic, like when I catch a glimpse of my reflection while cleaning the Phillips' pool.

I feel a third hand—this one at the front of my towel, searching. It slips under the edge, crossing a line I didn't offer. Heat floods my body, sharp and uninvited, like a spark catching dry skin. The beast in the darkness has many hands, many mouths, all reaching when something young wanders in. But it's too much. I shove backward, pushing through limbs and bodies I can't see, stumbling toward the dark gap I came through.

I'm running again. Last time, it was from the lumberjack at The Anvil. This time, it's from the part of me that keeps pretending this helps.

I take a long, hot shower to scrub off whatever the darkroom left behind. Part of me wants to release the tension, to shake off the madness that's been building all night. But I don't. Instead, I grab a clean towel, wrap it around my waist, and head back into the hallway.

A few silhouettes move about without urgency. A man in a mesh jock leans against the wall, arms crossed. Another lingers by the room he rented, leaning against the open door and watching men pass, reaching out to touch those he wishes would enter. It's like a spider perched on the fringe of its web.

I don't look at their faces. I don't want their names.

I continue down the hallway; the first man I pass is older, maybe fifty. He makes eye contact and follows me for a moment. I stop at a drinking fountain as he brushes past, trailing his fingers along the wall. I don't engage.

A tall man nods as I pass. Older, built like he spends every weekday at the gym. He brushes his hand against my arm when we cross in the narrow hallway. I don't stop, though. Not yet.

Another man, muscular in his early thirties, meets me near the sauna. He raises his chin and motions with his head. I don't speak—I turn and follow him to a dark corner. We stand for a moment, not quite touching each other. I nod once, and that's all he needs.

He presses against me—his hands at my waist, his mouth near my ear. I let him kiss me. It's dry, obligatory. I turn around, my back to his chest, and let him search under the towel. There's no connection. No words, just the ritual of touch that means nothing. It's not tender, but tender doesn't live in these rooms and hallways. He finishes quickly—I feel the sudden warmth and pull away, still untouched, still distant. He wipes his hands on the towel and disappears. It's not about pleasure—it's about surrender— but surrender on my terms. My mind is beginning to blank, and that's what I think I came for.

In the steam room, I sit for a while, letting the heat burn off everything I don't want to feel. A figure enters through the mist— forty maybe, a hairy chest with one pierced nipple. He sits across from me, legs wide, towel slipping open. Our eyes meet, and he gestures, but I shake my head. It's the small, universal signal that means "not tonight." I stay anyway, watching without seeing, running my hand across my chest in slow, suggestive gestures as if I'm trying to feel something that I don't.

I wander back to the small hallway leading to the video lounge, where a dozen men, half-dressed or fully nude, sit on the sofa or linger in the shadows, eyes fixed on the flickering screen and each other. The film plays without pause, and not a word is spoken. Whatever anyone's here for, no one admits it—not out loud.

I sit among them, eyes fixed on the flickering screen, letting the images blur into background noise. Someone shifts beside me, closer than necessary. Another figure moves in front of me, expectant. I don't respond. My body reacts on its own, like muscle memory without meaning. I close my eyes and try to disappear. But after a few minutes, the weight of it all settles in—the room, the silence, the why of it—and I rise to leave.

I haven't found what I'm looking for, yet I haven't shaken what I'm running from either.

Fatigue begins to set in, and I think about showering to leave. No clocks are on the wall, and time is hard to sense. It comes and goes in phases: a time to hunt, a time to submit, a time to dominate, and a time to disappear.

I walk toward the showers, down the long hallway of doors, when I spot him—a young, slim boy with warm skin and a nervous smile. There's an accent when he murmurs something I don't catch, soft and uncertain. He's leaning against the open door of his room. He's cute, and I nod. That's all it takes for him to invite me in.

The room smells faintly of poppers and sex, but it doesn't matter. The guy tries to kiss me, but I turn my face. I don't want tenderness here, not from him. Thwarted from kissing, he lowers himself to his knees in front of me instead. The boy gazes up, waiting for permission. I give it with a nod. He lowers himself and takes over—eager, practiced, his hands firm, his breath hot. I close my eyes and let it happen. Not for pleasure. For escape. It's not a conversation. It's a transaction.

Then I push him off and pull him to his feet. His mouth opens, breathy and eager, but whatever he calls me twists something in me. It's a name I never asked for, never claimed. It hits wrong, sharp under my skin. I'm not here to play a role. I'm not here to be someone's fantasy.

I take hold of his hips and turn him. He braces against the mattress, reaching for the lube on the bed, but I get there first. My chest presses against his back as I uncap the bottle, the gel cold on my fingers. I move without speaking—focused, mechanical, not tender.

The boy thinks he knows what's coming—wants it rough, wants me to play a part he's imagining. He keeps moaning, grinding back against me, pleading in breathless fragments. He reaches behind himself, trying to take control, to guide me where he wants me. I bat his hand away instead. Then I grip his waist, lift him clean off the floor, and toss him onto the bed. He scrambles to reposition—on hands and knees, still offering—but I grab his ankles and flip him onto his back instead.

He lies back, already aroused, one leg shifting open in invitation. But I press his knees together and guide them down flat. Then I straddle him, reach behind to steady myself, and lower myself, letting the space between us close—slowly, deliberately—until our bodies touch, every motion intentional, every breath controlled.

There's surprise in his eyes, but no resistance. I'm taller, heavier, and stronger. I take the lead—controlling the rhythm, keeping the moment on my terms. He adjusts beneath me, breath catching, yet still unsure. When he tries to move in response, I place a hand on his chest. "Don't," I say firmly, and he quiets, eyes wide, breath hitching.

I reach around, letting my hand slide between us—exploring, not rushing. His breath hitches, eyes fluttering as I apply steady pressure. He shifts beneath me, responding to my touch without words, his body giving in with a sharp, sudden gasp. I watch his head tip back, mouth open, every muscle drawn tight before he exhales all at once.

He reaches to touch me, but I knock his hand aside—once, then again—controlling the pace, the space between us. Finally, I catch his wrist and guide it gently to the mattress, holding it there—not forcefully, but firmly—as I move in closer, setting the rhythm of what comes next. He stays quiet beneath me, breath shallow, gaze fixed, like he's letting himself be led.

It builds like an orchestra—layers of breath and motion rising together, pressure and rhythm stacking into something almost symphonic until his whole body tightens. I hold him steady as the tension crests and breaks. He jerks beneath me, breath catching as the climax overtakes him. He sinks into the sheets he's clutching, trembling through silent waves of release.

His eyes stay shut, chest still heaving. He reaches for me again, but I'm already off the bed, pulling the towel around my waist as if none of it touched me, as if I wasn't there. I don't linger. I turn the knob and slip out before he can say a word.

The edges blur until I'm nothing but muscle and breath and need. This isn't pleasure—it's disappearance. I'm not chasing connection—I'm trying to vanish from it.

In the shower, I try to find some kind of release, but when it comes, it's muted—more a flicker than a flood. The pressure lifts, but it leaves behind the same hollow ache I walked in with. Whatever I was running from is still here, lingering in the steam and silence.

Places like this aren't about being seen. You slip through shadows, swap silence for contact, and leave more empty than you arrived. I don't feel proud. I don't feel ashamed, either. Just misplaced. Just somewhere else.

I dress in silence, avoiding the mirror as if it might accuse me. When I step outside, I breathe in the cool night air, but it doesn't help.

The receipt with Kevin's number remains in my back pocket. I don't take it out. Not yet.

By the time I leave, it's nearly four in the morning. My legs ache, my mouth is dry, and my whole body hums like it's hollowed out and refilled with static.

On the drive home, I don't turn on the radio. I take a long way. Past the park. Past the strip where people are still spilling out of late-night diners. Past Mateo's bar, now dark, chairs flipped on tables.

I can't help but think about Naomi and how I told her I was too tired for dinner. I think about Mateo and telling him I was heading home. I think about Kevin, about how I almost dialed the number in my back pocket before grabbing my car keys.

Unlocking the door to my apartment, I step inside. The room is still warm; the bed is unmade. I pull the receipt from my back pocket and place it on the coffee table where I had it earlier. I look at it for a long moment before turning away.

Stripping in the dark, I crawl under the sheets. My skin still smells like other people, but I don't shower again. What would it wash off? I lie there in my cowardice, watching the fan blades turn, wondering what's left when the lights come on—and whether I just ran out of reasons not to call him.

10

THE CALL BACK

I wake just before noon, wrapped in the kind of warmth that feels like it's coming from inside you—leftover adrenaline burned off in sleep. My mouth is dry, my eyes sting, and my limbs feel cast from lead. I roll to one side, squint at the light pooling through the blinds, and decide not to move.

The apartment is silent, save for the low hum of the ceiling fan above. The receipt is still on the coffee table where I left it, Kevin's number folded neatly inside, untouched.

I drift for another hour, half-asleep, not dreaming, just suspended. Eventually, I get up. Not because I want to, but because I need to. The laundry basket is overflowing. I sort without thought, toss a load in, and wipe down the counters. I empty the trash, scrub the coffee pot, and rinse a mug I left too long in the sink. This movement is the closest thing I've had to prayer in months—like a ritual. If I keep cleaning, maybe I'll make enough space in the room to think clearly and make a decision.

By mid-afternoon, I'm standing at the kitchen sink when I hear a knock at the door. Then Naomi's voice, muffled but unmistakable: "You alive in there?"

Grabbing a dish towel, I wipe my hands and open the door.

She's dressed for the heat—a sleeveless top, loose denim shorts, and a paper bag from Pete's tucked under her arm.

Her eyes scan me. "You look... vertical."

"Don't be fooled," I say. "I'm still mostly dead inside. Come in."

She smirks. "Good. You could use some dying. Been a minute since you slowed down." She holds up the bag. "Chicken salad sandwich, extra pickles."

I take the bag. "Thanks."

Naomi scans the room. "You resting or hiding?"

"Both," I answer, inspecting the bag's contents and pulling the sandwich out. I can't remember the last time I ate. It was likely yesterday morning, yet I didn't feel hungry until now.

Naomi studies me again. No judgment, just that quiet calibration she does, figuring out how much truth I can carry without collapsing.

"You're allowed," she says. "Sometimes, the only way out is through your laundry pile."

I chuckle before realizing I'm only wearing boxer shorts in front of her. My thoughts have been elsewhere since getting out of bed.

"Nice day out," she says, nodding toward the window. "You wanna get dressed and walk in the park?"

"Mind if we take that walk tomorrow?" I answer, my mouth full of the bite of the sandwich I've just taken. "I'm kinda catching up on chores and want to finish."

"Yeah, sure," she says. "That sounds good. Plan on lunch so we can talk."

On her way out, Naomi taps the doorframe twice with her knuckles. "Don't overthink everything. Just rest today. It's okay to do nothing."

I nod, and she heads off down the stairs, humming a tune under her breath.

I finish the sandwich standing at the counter, then pull on a fresh T-shirt. I think about going out again. Maybe Burkhart's. Maybe The Anvil. Maybe somewhere new. I stand at the open closet door, staring at my shirts. What version of me do I want to send out there tonight? Which Daniel would they see? But nothing fits right in my mind. The idea of it makes my chest feel tight. I peel the T-shirt off and toss it aside. I'm not doing that again. Not tonight.

Instead, I sink into the couch, unfolding the soft blanket and tucking my feet under it. I flip through the channels. I'm not looking for anything particular; I'm just trying to fill the quiet. I look for something old, warm, and familiar. I tell myself it's just background noise—a place to rest my eyes and disappear into something that isn't asking anything from me.

I land on *The Way We Were* just as it starts. I almost keep going, but something about the opening, Barbra Streisand's voice, sharp and certain, pulls me in. It's the kind of movie I'd pretend not to care about if someone else were in the room. But tonight, alone, I let it play. The grainy film stock, soft lighting, and ache that seem baked into every line are all too familiar. Two people who want each other but can't make it work. Love that never really leaves, even after it's already gone. I don't cry—I lie there, curled up on the couch, watching the flicker of a story I already know the ending to. I feel it settle over me like recognition.

The blanket feels somehow inadequate, as if it is missing weight. I shift on the couch and adjust the pillow, but the feeling doesn't go away. It's not the movie that gets me—it's the space beside me. The space I keep pretending doesn't matter. The space that stays empty no matter how many nights I fill with other bodies.

The folded receipt is still on the coffee table, a square of possibility I've been avoiding for two days. I stare at it, and the ache sharpens—not just for anyone, but for him.

Kevin.

Not the boy I left behind. Not the memory I've been feeding on. The man I saw two days ago—kind and real—was still able to look me in the eye. I don't move. I don't speak it aloud. I lie there, letting the truth sink in. I know exactly who I see beside me. *I want him.* I want to know if there's still something between us. I want to try.

And for the first time, I don't push that truth away.

I reach over to grab it, hold it, and let it live.

~

Naomi's knock comes just after ten—two short raps, then a pause. I'm already up, dressed, and halfway through making the bed. The apartment feels different this morning—the same furnishings and fan spinning overhead, but the silence isn't so loud. I open the door.

Naomi is in sunglasses and a tank top. Her hair is up, and she has an iced coffee in hand. She doesn't say hello; she eyes me head to toe and nods.

"Well damn," she says. "You're upright, dressed, and not brooding in the dark. That sandwich worked miracles."

I smirk. "Don't underestimate the power of pickles and sleep."

She narrows her eyes, like she's about to say something profound, but lets it go. Instead, she brushes past me and heads down the stairs. I fall into step like I always do.

The heat's not unbearable yet, just warm enough to make the air feel heavy in your lungs. We cut through a few shaded streets, then hit the trail loop in the park. There's quiet between us, but it's not awkward. Naomi never makes silence feel like a test.

Halfway through the loop, we veer toward Pete's at The Park. We find a table on the patio under the awning, with slatted metal chairs and peeling green paint. The fan above us clicks as it spins. Naomi orders eggs, bacon, and grits, and I go for eggs benedict again. It's starting to become a theme.

"You look better today," she says, stirring her coffee. "Still kind of ghostly, but less... haunted Victorian widow."

"Progress," I say, picking at a piece of her bacon on her plate that has broken off.

She doesn't smile at that. She watches me for a second longer than usual. Then: "So you slept it all off?"

"I did."

"Dreams?"

I shake my head. "Just rest."

Naomi leans back in her chair and lets the silence settle again. Her eyes drift to the edge of the patio, where a dog is tied to a bike rack, sitting quietly, watching everything with focus.

"Ever notice how dogs never try to hide how they feel?" she asks.

I glance at her, confused.

"You've got that look," she adds. "Like you're sitting still, but something inside you keeps tugging at the leash."

I don't say anything right away. Just take another bite of my eggs and chew slowly.

"You don't have to tell me," she says, softer this time. "But whatever it is, you don't look so," she pauses, "frantic anymore. Just like you're waiting for something."

There's a window where I could tell her about running into Kevin. About the number. About the bar, the bathhouse, the movie that wrecked me. But I don't. Not because I'm hiding it, but because I'm not ready to hear myself say it out loud.

I could never tell her about the bathhouse. I don't regret it, but I'm not proud either. And the thing with Kevin—deciding I want to call him—is that it's too new. Too fragile.

Naomi knows me too well. She'd see right through it, slap a name on something I'm only beginning to face.

I nod. "I'll figure it out."

"I know you will," she says. "Just promise you won't lie to yourself."

We finish our food without rushing. The breeze lifts occasionally, bringing the smell of cut grass and charcoal. Someone down the hill is tossing a Frisbee. A kid shrieks as it sails past him.

On the walk home, Naomi lightly bumps her shoulder against mine. "You ever think about getting a dog?"

"I can't even keep a plant alive."

"Fair," she says, grinning.

She pauses on the second step of our building's front stairs and turns to look at me. "You do seem different today. Steadier."

I shrug. "Sleep and time heal all."

Naomi holds my gaze for a moment longer, then nods like she's known all along.

"I've got manuscript edits to ignore and dishes not to do," she says.

"Thanks for today."

Naomi taps the center of my chest with two fingers but doesn't say anything. She merely nods like she sees something I don't.

The receipt is still where I left it. But it doesn't feel like a weight now—it feels like a door I'm finally ready to knock on.

11

At Home

(Same Sunday, Not Far Away)

(Josh)

The house is quiet when I wake. No alarm, no sound except the distant rattle of the ice maker in the kitchen. I reach across the sheets and feel the space beside me—still warm, but barely. Kevin is already up.

I roll out of bed slowly, padding barefoot down the hall and into the kitchen. He's already at the small dining table, wearing his reading glasses, hunched slightly over a textbook with a pen balanced between his fingers. A half-drunk mug of coffee sits beside him next to a yellow legal pad covered in neat, angular handwriting.

"Morning, baby," I say.

Kevin glances up, then offers a soft smile. "Hey. Didn't mean to wake you."

"You didn't." I cross the room, kiss his temple, and glance at the legal pad.

The title at the top of the page is written in sharp, precise lettering: *Preliminary Market Update: Forecasting Client Behavior Post-Rollout—by Kevin Summers*. I smile at its formality as if he's already halfway to running his own department.

"What are you working on this time, Professor Summers?" I jokingly ask, leaning over to steal a sip of his coffee.

He glances up again, a small smile tugging at the corner of his mouth. "Just prepping for Tuesday."

Kevin's crew-cut hair is still damp from a quick rinse, and the tan of his skin stands out beneath the crisp white T-shirt stretched across his chest and arms. Kevin's always been solid, broad-shouldered, athletic, and clean-cut, making strangers assume they know him. But they don't.

"It's almost ten. Have you been at it long?"

"Since six-thirty."

He says it without complaint as if it's just what Sundays are for now—stats, theory, case studies. Since starting the MBA program at Emory, weekends have become his second shift.

We moved to Atlanta a year and a half ago so he could finish his undergraduate degree. Now he's full-time at IBM as a Junior Business Analyst, and every spare moment goes into this next phase. He never says it aloud, but I know he's making up for lost time.

I pour myself a cup of coffee and sit across from him. He reads for another minute, underlines something, and then finally looks up.

"Any plans today?"

I shrug. "Thought we could walk over to B-Side or maybe grab lunch in Little Five Points. Or not. I'm good either way."

Kevin smiles again, but it doesn't quite land. "Maybe later. I need to prepare for Tuesday's meeting. Rosenbaum's expecting a draft analysis by Monday night."

"Right," I say, even though I've never met Rosenbaum and have no idea what the draft is about. I sip my coffee and let the silence stretch.

It's not a cold silence—not distant, just routine. We've been renting this house in Virginia Highlands for three months now. We were ready for something quieter, closer to school, and more grounded: a yard, a porch, a real kitchen. We haven't unpacked everything yet, but the house feels more like us than living at The Mayfair, the Midtown high-rise we rented before. This feels like home.

"Hungry? I ask as I rise and walk to the kitchen, now that it appears we'll be staying in.

"Famished," he replies. "We can head to the park after this—maybe hit some balls?" he adds, still underlining and taking notes.

I set a plate near him. It's nothing fancy, just some eggs and a slice of toast, but I scratch something on a Post-it note and stick it on his plate: *Preliminary Meal Update: Forecasting Boyfriend Behavior Post-Breakfast—by Josh Bennett.* Kevin murmurs a thank you without noticing it, but when he does, he chuckles and looks up at me. He signals me closer with an index finger, and I bend toward him. He gently holds the back of my head and draws me nearer. He gives me a passionate kiss.

"You're the best, Chef Bennett," he says. "I love you."

"I love you, too, Professor Summers."

Kevin doesn't eat right away, though. His work consumes him: he reads, highlights, and takes notes. He's a man on a mission, not easily deterred by distractions.

I watch him from the kitchen as I clean up, his jaw flexing as he reads, his brow slightly furrowed. He's always focused like this: methodical, intent. It's part of what I love about him. I know he's not pulling away. He's just doing what he's always done: building the next version of himself brick by brick.

When I bring him a refill, I set the mug down and let my fingers brush his shoulder. It startles him. Just slightly. Barely a flinch. But enough.

"Sorry," I say quickly. "Didn't mean to—"

"It's okay," he says, setting his pen down and leaning back. He rubs the side of his neck like he's just now realizing how tight he's been holding himself. "I guess I'm a little on edge."

"Busy week?" I ask.

"Yeah."

The air between us isn't tense, but it's not as easy as usual. Still, it's comfortable and familiar. There's love in the silence—we've grown used to living in its corners lately.

We move to the living room, and Kevin carries his books and notes to the sofa. I grab my sketchpad and sit nearby, letting the quiet settle again. The house still smells faintly of roasted coffee and laundry detergent—clean and lived in. Several half-unpacked boxes sit near the bookshelf. Three months now, and we still haven't found the time to place everything.

My job at the rehab center keeps me busy enough—outpatient therapy for mostly older clients recovering from strokes, surgeries, or accidents. I like the work. It's hands-on, physical, but still full of care. Some days, I think it's the only thing keeping me sane when Kevin disappears into his work, classes, books, and spreadsheets.

When we first met, it was in a parking lot outside a club in Bayview. Kevin was still reeling from everything he'd lost in a too-young marriage gone bad too quickly. He was only then beginning to figure himself out. I didn't know any of that at the time. I just knew he looked tired and out of place and somehow familiar. We didn't even go back inside. He said no to coffee that night but gave me his number. A week later, we spent five hours talking at a diner. That was four years ago, and the start of all this.

Kevin's satchel, lugged back and forth between work and school, slouches near the entryway. When the pager inside goes off, the high-pitched chirp slices through our home's calm like a fire alarm. Kevin flinches. So do I.

"What the hell was that?" I ask, already rising halfway off the couch.

"Sorry." He sighs and crosses the room, digging through the side pocket until he finds the small black device. He flips it over, squinting at the numbers.

"Nothing," he says, clicking it off. "Just a page. No code."

"Work?" I ask.

"Doubt it. We use priority codes—two-digit tags for urgency. And they never page on Sundays." He drops the pager back into his bag and zips it shut. "Don't recognize the number, anyway. I've gotten a few of those. I guess it used to belong to a doctor, probably still rerouted from an answering service."

"You want to call back?"

Kevin shakes his head. "Naw. If it's urgent, they'll page back.

I go back to sketching. Kevin goes back to reading. The quiet holds, and the light through the window shifts as the afternoon passes.

"Hey," he says, closing his book and rubbing his eyes. "Do you still want to walk down to the park? My eyes are shot, and I could use a break."

"Yeah," I say, standing. "Let's get some fresh air."

Kevin nods, already reaching for his keys. He doesn't look back. But I do—just once—at the satchel slouched in the corner, still zipped shut.

12

THE LUNCH ENCOUNTER

I call from the back warehouse at the shop, where the only air-conditioning vent rattles like it's working overtime. I'm on break, flipping through the carbon copies of the day's route sheets. The linoleum beneath my boots is sticky in spots, as if someone had spilled a Coke three weeks ago and never cleaned it up. A faint whiff of chlorine clings to everything back here—sweat, chemicals, and rust.

It's Monday, late morning, and my fingers sweat against the plastic phone receiver. I dial the number Kevin gave me again. I don't expect him to pick up—and he doesn't. The line blares its sequence of beeps and tones, cold and mechanical, just as it did yesterday.

With the receiver pressed to my ear, I listen but hear nothing. Then it hits: Kevin gave me a fake number. Not by accident. Not because he forgot. On purpose. A clean exit without having to say the words. I set the phone down carefully as if it might accuse me of something. My stomach twists—not with anger, but something smaller. Shame, maybe. Or that familiar sting of wanting more than someone else ever did. The only one still chasing ghosts. Maybe I made Kevin into something he never was—maybe I always do that.

I'm still staring at the phone when it suddenly rings—loud, sharp, like a slap. I flinch and snatch it up before it can go off again.

"Sunbelt Pool and Spa, this is Daniel."

There's a brief pause—static and breath—then, "Hey. It's me. Kevin." His voice is like rain on hot pavement: calm and unrushed, like he has no idea I was seconds away from writing him off.

I lean back in the creaking chair, my heart pounding like a dropped wrench in an empty metal bucket. "You've got good timing," I say, trying to sound casual. "Another thirty seconds, and I was gonna chuck your number in the trash."

Kevin chuckles, soft and low. "Yeah, I'm sorry. I was in a meeting and had to find a quiet place to make a call. It's a work pager that only shows your number. Long story."

"Uh-huh." I force a smirk into my voice. "Sure. Thought you gave me a fake number, or maybe you changed your mind."

"I wouldn't do that," he says—then, after a pause: "Not to you."

He says it like he means it, and just like that, the disappointment rewires itself into something lighter. Not quite relief, not yet, but the panic and ache ease.

"Catch you at a bad time?" I ask.

"No, it's fine," Kevin says. "It's just that I'm at work."

I glance around at the sun-faded posters for chlorine tablets and pool vacuums. "Me too."

"Hey, but I'm glad you called. It's been a long time, buddy," he says. I can almost hear the smile in the way he says it. "Hang on."

On Kevin's end, there's the muffled clunk of a door and a sudden hush. I picture him stepping into his office or a conference room for privacy. There's a faint rustle—papers or keys maybe—and then it's just him.

"Okay," he says. "How have you been?"

70

I hesitate, twisting the phone cord around my fingers. "Good, real good. I just wanted to say hi. I can't believe we ran into each other last week. I had no idea you were up here in Atlanta."

Kevin pauses.

"I'm okay," he says. "Staying busy." He sounds like someone who is half in another room—even if he's alone.

"Say, you eat lunch yet?" I ask. Then I look at the clock on the wall. It's 10:30 a.m., and I feel stupid.

"No, not yet," he chuckles.

"Want to?" I add. "Today?"

He hesitates again. Then: "Yeah. Sure. Meet at Ansley, the same place as last week? Say, 12:30?"

~

By the time I arrive, the sun's baking the brick walls of the courtyard. I've changed into a clean pale blue polo without the Sunbelt logo stitched on the chest. I pretend I didn't do it to look better, sitting on the same bench near where we ran into each other last week, trying not to look at every man walking by like he might be Kevin.

When he does show up, he's wearing fitted khakis and a white button-down rolled at the sleeves, his IBM tote slung over one shoulder. A subtle, clean scent trails behind him—some blend of soap, cologne, and office air. He spots me and gives me a smile and a slight nod.

"Hey," he says, stepping closer. "Thanks for waiting."

"Would've waited longer," I reply, standing.

71

We head toward the sub shop at the back corner of the figure-eight-shaped row of shops and businesses to escape the heat and comings and goings of people in the parking lot out front. It smells like sliced tomatoes, ham, pickles, and warm bread. Kevin glances around, then picks a table near the back, slightly away from the windows.

"How long do we have?" he asks.

What immediately comes to my mind is forever, but I don't say that. "My next client is at two, and it's nearby, so I'm good for a while. You?"

"Great," he smiles. "No, I've got time. I know I'll be there for a while tonight. I have a big meeting tomorrow, so there's lots to prepare for."

We order sandwiches and iced teas, and when the food arrives, we unwrap our lunches with the crinkle of wax paper and the clink of plastic cutlery. The bread is warm from the press. The mustard stings the back of my nose, sharp and bright.

"So you're in the pool game?" Kevin asks, taking a bite of his roast beef.

"Yeah," I say. "Mostly field stuff, which I love, but stuck in the office sometimes scheduling, ordering supplies, shit like that."

Kevin nods. "Well, you always did love the water. Sunbelt, right?"

"Impressed you remembered."

Kevin smirks. "Hard to forget a company name with a palm tree in the logo, especially when it's sitting on *your* chest."

A flicker runs through me—just enough to notice. Kevin says it playfully as if we never missed a beat. It's nothing on the surface. Just a smile, a memory. But it lands somewhere deeper, like a match brushing too close to paper that's already dry. I don't look up right away. If I do, he'll see it. The ache. The hope. That part of me is still waiting for someone to say I matter.

I take a drink of my tea. The ice clinks, and the taste is sweet and metallic against my tongue.

"How'd you end up here?" It's only one of a hundred things I want to know.

"Well, I came up to finish school at Emory—just started grad school part-time," he says. "MBA. I joined an internship program with IBM, and I'm now a full-time junior analyst. I mostly swim in data and spreadsheets, though. Not romantic."

'Romantic.' I repeat the word in my head. "So you really did become the guy I used to make fun of," I tease.

He grins. "And you're still the guy who made fun of me."

We laugh. It's light and real. The people and sounds in the deli fade for a second—the fluorescent buzz, the register's ping, the scent of garlic pickles—it all fades, and it's just us. Our knees almost touch under the table.

I keep watching his hands. The way he moves. He's still careful and precise—the kind of guy who wipes the crumbs off the table before he's even done eating.

Neither of us brings up that night. Not yet. The receipt in my pocket feels heavier by the minute, but I don't reach for it.

As we finish, Kevin glances at his watch. "I should head back."

"Me too," I say, though I don't want to. "Same time tomorrow?"

He looks at me. I can sense the surprise on his face at my question, the initial reaction of fear or perhaps caution, and the pull of desire to reply with agreement. "Yeah," he begins, "tomorrow's a stretch. That big meeting is going to be a killer."

"I'll buzz your pager in the morning," I say before he can say no. "You know—just in case."

Kevin pauses, then smiles. He says 'no,' but I hear 'maybe'— and I'm already hoping for 'yes.'

Outside, the heat wraps around us again. Kevin turns to go, and I watch him walk away, past the workout he skipped and into the parking lot, that solid frame disappearing into the brightness of the day.

My shirt sticks to my back. The tea is gone. The taste of mustard still lingers—sharp, unexpected, like a question that doesn't fade just because no one answered it.

I'm already thinking about what to say next time—what not to say—and whether next time will even come.

13

INVITATION TO SWIM

The air tastes like dust and copper as I climb back into the company pickup, sweat and grime soaked into the collar of my shirt. It's almost five. The sun's still high, baking the asphalt in the service lot behind the office, where the smell of hot rubber and motor oil clings to everything. The engine cuts off, and the door slams harder than intended.

Inside, the front desk is quiet, and I notice tomorrow's route sheets jammed into everyone's trays. I nod at Janice, the receptionist, who waves me over with one hand while the other holds the phone against her shoulder.

"Guy called for you earlier," she says, handing me a slip of paper.

A glance down: a name, a number, and a pang in my chest. I recognize the number as Kevin's office.

"Said he might be calling back later," she adds, tucking a pencil behind her ear. "He sounded cute."

"Thanks," I reply, folding the paper into my back pocket like it might fly away if I'm not careful.

Back in my apartment, the window unit hums in the background, pushing cool air into the room. I kick off my boots and step into the bathroom to splash cold water on my face. My reflection in the mirror looks flushed and unsteady.

Drying off with the edge of a clean towel, I knock gently on the wall between our apartments; two quick taps, a pause, then two more taps.

A beat later, she cracks the door, her phone in hand. "You wanna borrow it? Five bucks," she jokes.

"How about five minutes," I say. "Promise."

"Who you gonna call?"

I pause. "My Granny," I say. "It's her birthday."

"Ahh-ha. How old is Granny?"

"Very old," I reply.

She squints as if she doesn't believe me, but hands the phone over anyway.

The wire connecting the phone to the wall plate is extra long. She likes to use the phone in any number of locations throughout the apartment when talking to clients: in the living room, the kitchen, the bedroom, and even while soaking in the tub or sitting on the toilet—it depends on her mood and how much of her attention the client requires at that particular time.

"No long distance," she says, rolling her eyes and muttering something about me being shady before closing her door. The long, cream-colored cord snakes behind me, trailing beneath her door and under mine atop the hardwood floors. The cord trails into my apartment as I shut the door quietly behind me.

The receiver smells faintly of Naomi's coconut lotion as I sit cross-legged on the floor, back against the bed. Each digit dials slowly, like spelling out a confession.

It rings twice. "This is Kevin. May I help you?"

"Hey," I say, heartbeat in my throat. "It's me. Daniel."

"Hi there." He sounds relaxed, as if he has just leaned back in his chair, ready to end a long day at the office. There's a faint sound of paper shuffling behind him. "Thanks for calling back. Sorry, I had to leave a message at your work. I wasn't sure if you'd given me your home number or if I had misplaced it."

"No, work is fine. I just don't usually give out this one." I didn't want to tell Kevin that I still didn't have a home phone after a year of living here. Not yet, at least. I also didn't want him calling Naomi.

He pauses. "Well, I'm glad you called back."

I glance at the phone cord stretching under the door and lower my voice.

"I don't have long," I say. "But I've been thinking about the other day."

"Me too," his voice softens. "I was wondering if you wanted to meet again. Maybe do something less random."

My mouth goes dry. A nod—then a reminder that Kevin can't see it. "Yeah. Sure." I try to keep the excitement out of my voice. "That sounds good."

"You free Friday afternoon?" he asks. "Emory has a pretty nice Aquatic Center on campus with an awesome pool. It's pretty quiet on Fridays, especially later in the afternoon."

"I could be free."

"Maybe three?" he suggests.

"Three works." My mind speeds ahead of my words, thinking about my regular Friday route. I'm usually at the Phillips' around two, so I'll have to be quick with the morning regulars. I consider simply asking for Friday afternoon off, but then dismiss the thought. We're in the height of the summer season, and I know how busy we are. I know what the answer to requesting time off would be. No, it's better not to ask. Hopefully, nothing new drops in my Friday box.

A moment of quiet spins out between us, not uncomfortable, just full.

"All right," Kevin says finally. "I'll see you then, Daniel."

"See you there," I echo.

We both hang up slowly, like we're not ready to. A few more seconds pass sitting on the floor, listening to the low hum of the AC and the slight creak of Naomi's floorboards next door. The scent of coconut lotion still clings to the receiver.

I feel a couple of tugs on the phone cord from the other end. I doubt Naomi urgently needs her phone back. It's been barely over five minutes, and she's already messing with me.

I haven't told her. I need to.

If Kevin calls this number back and I'm not there—

No. I didn't give Kevin the number. I said I don't usually give it out. That's true. True enough.

The cord gives another tug from Naomi's end.

I unplug the cord from the phone's base. The next time Naomi tugs at it, I chuckle in amusement—the sight of the cord whipping back beneath her door with no tension, no phone attached to it.

As quietly as possible, I place her uncorded telephone in the hallway in front of 3C.

I'll tell her soon. I will.

14

GHOSTS AND SECOND CHANCES

I'm off early, but I don't sit still. The second I'm home, I start moving around the apartment like someone's coming over—folding laundry, cleaning the kitchen, mopping floors, and wiping the streaks from the bathroom mirror. I even shave. Not that it's needed, but the ritual calms me. Clean lines. Fresh start. All of this has nothing to do with meeting Kevin to swim tomorrow, of course.

Sunlight filters through the oak leaves outside my window, casting flickering shadows across the floor as I mop, like ripples scattering light across the bottom of a pool when I stir the water with my brush. I clip my nails and toss the trimmings. Change shirts twice. Stupid, I know. I'm not going anywhere. Not tonight, anyway.

A knock at the door—two firm raps.

Unlocking it reveals Naomi, one brow raised, as if she just caught me doing something I shouldn't.

"Nice move with the phone cord yesterday, asshole."

"What?" I blink. No clue what she's talking about.

"You ready to eat?" she asks, stepping inside without waiting.

"Gimme one second," I say, grabbing my shoes. She takes a slow look around the place—clocks the clean counters and the fresh shirt—but doesn't say a word.

It's thick outside. Summer buzzes from every tree, and the sidewalk feels sticky under our shoes. Naomi is wearing a tank top and a long, flowing skirt that moves like sails catching the heat. We pass the playground, the stone pavilion, and the art students sketching on benches as we head toward Pete's. It's one of Naomi's go-to restaurants, probably her favorite, where she can eat healthy and people-watch from their covered outdoor patio.

The patio is half full, and overhead fans oscillate above our table to cut the heat. The iced teas arrive quickly, their glasses already sweating, with lemon slices floating like lazy pieces of the sun.

Naomi takes one sip, then cuts her eyes at me. "So. Who were you on the phone with last night?"

I nearly choke on my drink. "Jesus. Did you listen to the wall with a glass to your ear?"

"Nope. Just heard your dumbass whispering like a spy sneaking state secrets. So who was it?"

I shrug. "Nobody."

She leans forward. "So nobody has a name now?"

"It was just a call. Someone I used to know."

She narrows her eyes. "Someone, or the someone from last week?"

The spoon clinks against ice as I stir my tea. "You sound like my mom."

Naomi smirks. "Please. Your mama would be glad you're talking to someone who doesn't live in your pants. But I'm not your mama, baby. I'm the one who has to clean you up when this goes sideways. I'm just trying to figure out why you're acting like a teenager sneaking out the window. You normally drag guys in and spit 'em out like chicken bones once you've had your fill."

"Come on. It's not like that."

She lets it sit a beat. "You've been different since that brunch. Quiet, but jittery, like you got static under your skin. Now, suddenly, you've got electricity flowing between your fingers, cleaning your place up like the Queen of England herself is about to visit. Ever since that phone call."

I sigh and sit back, then offer her a bone. "We ran into each other. We're catching up. It's not a big deal."

Naomi studies me over the rim of her glass. "Yeah, I knew it." She leans back, not angry but weary of watching this story unfold. "Baby, I don't care who he is—if you've gotta hide him, that's not love. That's a warning."

The air between us shifts. It's not heavy yet, but it cools. Naomi knows. She doesn't say his name, but she knows.

"You're gonna do what you're gonna do," she adds. "Just don't pretend like I didn't warn you."

We eat in pieces. I push my fries around the plate more than I eat them. Naomi talks about a client who tipped her with coupons. I laugh where I'm supposed to. Then we sit quietly again.

Mateo shows up near the end, dressed in what he'll wear to tend bar tonight and with an easy grin that makes strangers stare. He kisses Naomi's cheek before sliding into the chair between us.

She looks directly at Mateo and blurts out, "Did you know Daniel is talking to that guy from Bayview again? Have you been encouraging him?"

Mateo hasn't hit his seat yet, his hands grasping the arms of his chair as if considering whether he should sit or walk away now. He glances my way as if looking for the answer.

"Ummm," he begins to speak, "what are we discussing?"

"You know damn well what we're talking about," she barks back as if it's all his fault. "Our boy here is trading truth for a fantasy—that Kevin guy from the past. And he knows the guy has a boyfriend." She turns to look at me again. "Nope, not me. Ghosts don't haunt; they seduce. I've seen this movie before, baby child. You won't like the ending."

"Well," Mateo says, fanning himself with the menu, "aren't we a moody little picnic this evening?"

Naomi gives him a look. "It's the heat."

"Sure," he says, eyes flicking between us. "Nothing sizzles like shade."

We laugh, but mine feels off. Naomi's already halfway home in her head.

When we leave, she doesn't loop her arm through mine like usual. We walk side by side, but it feels like we're already back in our separate apartments. We reach her door, and she pauses.

"Look, baby," Naomi says calmly, "just make sure you're not calling a ghost a second chance. You'll be disappointed and get hurt. Call if you need anything."

I nod as the key turns in the lock. "But I'll need to borrow your phone to call you," smiling for levity.

"Jerk," I hear as she steps into 3C and shuts the door.

I stand in my entryway, staring at the closed door between us.

I haven't told her everything: about our past together and our plans to meet tomorrow. I don't dare.

But I'm starting to think she already knows. And the thing is— if she's right, I won't be able to say I didn't see it coming.

15

THE RIPPLE EFFECT

The Phillips house comes into view almost an hour earlier than usual, and even that feels too late. Morning appointments were a blur—done well, but without pause, working through lunch in anticipation of meeting Kevin at three.

Bag in hand, I let myself in through the side gate. The latch sticks, as always. The backyard is quiet, the same polished postcard it always is—perfect hedges, a blue pool like a mirror, and the breeze barely nudging the trees around the yard's edges. There's no sign of Patrick, which is a good thing today.

I hustle around the perimeter, checking the pump first, then the skimmer. Everything looks fine. I start the filter and brush the shallow end, working fast but precisely. I've done this a hundred times, maybe more. Today, it's just another appointment, not with my favorite client or in my favorite pool on my route. Today, I need to get somewhere else—where I want to be—the Aquatic Center of Emory's campus at three o'clock to meet Kevin.

No time to overthink what it means or might be. It's just a swim, I tell myself. Two guys who used to know each other. Old friends. Nothing more.

But that's a lie. I shaved this morning and brought my good polo to change into. I keep checking my watch as if three o'clock would arrive sooner if I kept looking at it.

The sun is brutal, heat curling off the stone deck. Sweat's already sliding down my spine. The shirt comes off, and I toss it onto the chair under the umbrella. The breeze finds my skin, cooling it under the sweat. I keep brushing—long, slow strokes—a repetition that calms your body when your head is elsewhere.

The pool water shimmers with every pass, scattering light across the plaster walls beneath the surface like I paint the bottom with ripples. A pause, just long enough to watch it dance. Something about it slows me down. I lean in—the smell of the breeze blowing against the surface, the sound of water against the tile, the hypnotic repetition of the brush along the bottom.

And then I'm somewhere else.

~

(Four Years Earlier)

Running into Kevin that night at the convenience store is a fluke—him getting gas and me killing time. He calls my name, and I momentarily freeze. Still, I recognize the voice, his name tumbling out of my mouth to greet him like muscle memory. We exchange pleasantries and chat briefly. He invites me over. And just like that, we're friends again, like no time has passed, yet the echo of everything we never said lingers between us.

His aunt Alice is snoring loudly, curled up on the couch with the TV flickering in front of her and some knitted blanket tucked around her feet. Kevin whispers, and I follow him, laughing because I don't know what else to do with myself. The second Kevin mentions the pool, I'm halfway through the door. The Florida night air is thick and warm, and I throw my sandals off to dip my toes into the water. It's like bathwater, like summer. "Hell yeah," I say. "Let's get smashed and see who can do the best jack-knife."

Kevin gives me that crooked smile. "I'll pass on getting smashed," he says. "And we both know who'd win, Mr. Swim Team."

"Old man," I mutter under my breath. Being on the Swim and Dive team is what I miss most about high school. It's the only thing I miss, and I welcome the chance to get into the water.

"Room's through the kitchen on the right. Swim trunks are on the closet shelf. Grab a pair while I get some towels."

I grab one off the shelf, and my hand hesitates just a second before I strip down and pull the black Speedo up my legs. When I return to the patio, Kevin's already in the water.

"Watch your head," he calls out.

I don't slow down. I sprint toward the edge and leap over Kevin's head, slicing into the water in a smooth, horizontal dive, like I'm still seventeen and none of this matters. I resurface with a shake of my hair that sends streams of water flying toward him.

"Wow, that feels fantastic!"

"Didn't your mom warn you about diving into the shallow end?" Kevin asks.

"She warned me about lots of things," I shoot back. "Didn't listen to any of 'em."

He tosses me a beer, and I float on my back, balancing the bottle on my stomach like a lazy otter with a shell. It rocks gently with the movement of the water, and I realize how easy it is to be here, right now, in the night air, with him.

We float and talk, but not about anything important. Kevin teases me about Stacy, and I joke about what a bitch she is, how stupid I was to get married so young, and how little time it took to become so miserable. Underneath the sarcasm, however, there's an ache. I don't know why I'm saying any of it. Maybe I want him to ask the real questions. Perhaps I want him to see through me.

I pull the classic submarine beer trick—drink the whole bottle underwater, then let it rocket to the surface, filled with the air from my lungs. Kevin laughs, and something inside me loosens again.

We dive and splash, wrestle for sunken quarters like kids, like idiots. It doesn't matter. I want him to laugh. I want to feel good again.

After a while, we drift toward the shallow end and lean our necks against the pool's edge, floating on our backs, our chests bobbing above the water. We let our breath slow, and our bodies relax, staring up at the stars overhead—quiet now, the space between us calm again.

"I'm so fucked up," I say before I can stop myself.

He turns to look at me. "You shouldn't drink so much, then."

"Not the beer, man." I stare at the stars, counting none of them. "My life."

Kevin doesn't argue. He just listens.

I tell him how I feel stuck. About marrying someone I barely liked. About working at my dad's restaurant and waking up every day like I've already screwed it all up.

"Your life isn't fucked up," Kevin says. "You're still a baby, for Christ's sake." He tells me I can change things, that people make mistakes and learn from them, and that it's never too late. It sounds good, but I'm not sure if I believe him. It's so easy for him. Kevin never makes mistakes. I should have done what he did and gone to college. He's always been perfect at everything.

I don't tell him what I want to say—that seeing him tonight feels like something cracking open inside me again.

Instead, I tell him the story about the waiter at my dad's restaurant who hit on me. I ask Kevin if it means something—that I didn't get mad at the guy—that I didn't say I was straight, but instead told him I was engaged. As I tell the story, I shift uncomfortably in the water, suddenly aware of how exposed I feel in his borrowed Speedo—where our attention drifts.

I glance to the side when I realize what's happening, but Kevin doesn't flinch. He's not joking or getting weird. He's listening—and he's staring at my bulge, making it even more pronounced. I think about ending my float, ducking underwater, but I don't. I can't—frozen in place by how it makes me feel inside, the way desire feels, both sides of it. I can't move. I don't want to move.

I catch him blink, and I think he's suddenly becoming aware that his gaze lingered too long. He quickly looks at my face, but it's too late. I've already shifted my glance back to the stars. I'm not sure if he's caught me noticing him, but I take a deep breath to recenter my focus as he does the same.

"So," Kevin finally says, "if you weren't mad, you think a part of you wanted to?"

"No," I answer, glancing back at him. "I wouldn't want to with him." I could tell he sensed the emphasis land hard and clear."

We turn in the water and let our arms and elbows rest on the pool's edge, our chins atop our wrists as our bodies hang relaxed and limp under the water's surface. We are closer to one another now, and our elbows touch briefly as we lower our voices, as if afraid someone might overhear our words.

"So," Kevin says softly. "Have you ever thought about being with any *other* guy?"

"I don't know." I take a deep breath. "I mean, I've wondered. You know, not like wanted to, or tried to, or anything. But yeah. I've wondered." I ask him if he thinks that's creepy.

"Of course not," he replies. He says everyone has wondered—it's part of figuring yourself out. He says everyone is on a sexual spectrum, like other traits, and no one is one hundred percent anything. Anyone who says they haven't thought about it is lying. I believe him. Not because I need to, but because I want to.

"So," I say, testing the water further. "*You've* thought about having sex with a guy, then?"

He smirks. "Are you trying to entrap me in my own logic?"

"You said everyone, didn't you?"

"Okay, fine, if you must know. I have thought about it before. Yeah, sure I have."

"With anyone in particular?"

"No, not really, just in general." He doesn't dodge, but his eyes say otherwise.

"Did you ever do it?" I ask. I feel this buzz in my chest. Not from the beer. From the way he's watching me now.

"No," he says. "But I don't think I'd feel bad or guilty if I had."

There's a quiet and dangerous pause between us.

Kevin tells me that if two people have feelings for each other, whether of the same or opposite sex, they should be allowed to express those feelings. "Besides," he laughs, "sex is sex, and sex is supposed to be fun. What's the big deal?"

"So you think you ever will?" I ask.

"What, have sex with a guy? I don't know. Sure. Maybe. I don't know." He turns away from me to gaze into the darkness of the yard's corner, where the pool lights don't shine and vulnerability lives. "If I did," he continued, "it would have to be with someone I knew, someone I trusted and felt comfortable with. Someone I had feelings for."

There was another long silence. The water was placid and grew warmer as the conversation shifted.

"So," I ask, "do you have feelings for *me*?"

Kevin turns. "Why, Daniel! Are you propositioning me?"

My heart pounded under the water. I couldn't tell if Kevin was teasing or testing me—maybe both. It was like a silent dare.

"I don't know," I replied. "Do you want to be propositioned?"

We are playing a game of cat and mouse—a dangerous one. Neither wants to tip our hand first nor go too far, fearing we may not be able to recover our dignity.

"Yes," Kevin says. "I like you. I've always enjoyed your company. I'm glad as hell we ran into one another tonight."

I give him a crooked grin. "Thanks, but that's not what I asked, is it?"

Kevin inhales, and this time doesn't dodge it. "You want me to say it?" he asks. "Fine. Yes, I would have sex with you." He is calm and says it plainly. "In fact," he adds, "I think we should."

I look at him. I'm not shocked. I'm just searching. "You really want to?"

"Yeah, why not?" he says. "We're both curious. We're alone. We're friends. I trust you. I feel comfortable with you. And I know this stays between us, right?"

My grin lingers. "You can trust me, and yeah, why not? I want to." The moment I say it, something shifts—not in the water, not in the air, but in me. I want him. And there it is, the horse is out of the barn, and I am relieved. Yes, it feels like being out on a limb and vulnerable, but I'm taking control of my desire and taking a chance, one of the few chances of free choice I have left. We both said it now. Both want it.

I sense our surroundings again—the warm night air, water, and pool light glowing softly beneath us, casting luminous shapes and shadows on our legs, torsos, and swimsuits. The space between us pulses with quiet energy, and I don't move. I just let it fill me.

"Hold on a second," he says, grabbing the pool's edge and slowly lifting himself out of the water. He pulls the sliding glass open and turns the patio lights off at the switch. We're cloaked in moonlight now, soft and silvery, shimmering off the surface while everything else disappears.

"There, that's better," he says. He lowers himself back into the water and moves slowly, carefully, and deliberately toward me. His hands land on either side of me against the pool edge, caging me in but not trapping me. He leans in, close but not touching. It is dark, late, and quiet; we both know we have privacy.

I don't move, not toward him or away—until I feel his lips brush against mine. It is soft and gentle, barely anything, like a whisper of a kiss. I see him back away an inch to read my reaction. Still, I don't move. I don't need to. Kevin knows. Our lips taste like pool water and intense longing. I smirk as I close my eyes once more.

Kevin leans in again, and this time, the kiss is the kind that breaks things open. He lets his hands drift to my back, slowly and cautiously, lowering them to my hips to draw me closer to him. The pool wall no longer holds me in place—Kevin does.

I rest my arms around his shoulders to let my body float into his embrace. I straddle him, wrapping my legs around his waist as we continue to kiss. Our bodies press together, our chests touch, and our arms wrap around each other in an embrace. The water engulfs us as we engulf each other—it rocks us gently as the heat and yearning between us swell.

"Are we going to do this here?" I whisper, my voice quivering slightly. It is dark, and I know we are alone, yet I feel uneasy about being out in the open, exposed as we are.

"No," Kevin says. "Let's go inside."

The water splashes onto the concrete deck as we lift ourselves out of the water and grab the towels from the patio chair. Kevin bends to dry off, and my gaze follows the way the moonlight moves with him: across the curves of his spine, the width of his shoulders, down his arms. He's always moved like someone sure of himself.

We wrap the damp towels around our waists and move through the sliding glass doors, our bare feet silent on the tile floor. Neither of us says a word as Kevin leads me toward his bedroom—the moment either of us can stop, but neither wants to.

~

"Hey, pool guy!"

The voice cuts across the water like a stone skipping on surface tension. I blink hard, and the pole slips from my hand—snapped back to the present. My knuckles ache from how tightly I've been gripping it.

"Can you hear me?"

I glance up. Patrick is standing under the patio awning, leaning against one of the columns with a half-eaten popsicle in one hand and a crooked smirk on his face. His hair is damp like he just got out of the shower, and he's wearing a towel low around his waist—nothing else, by the looks of it. He's more tanned now and looks unbothered, like some prince of summer who has already figured out that rules don't apply to him.

"Yeah," I call back, masking the heat in my face with a casual nod. "Sorry. Zoned out for a minute."

"You think?" he says, stepping off the patio and walking barefoot across the hot flagstone like it's nothing. "I've been standing here for a full minute. I thought you might fall in."

I wipe sweat from my forehead and hang the pole on the hooks beside the pump. "Just thinking."

"Looked more like feeling," he says, sucking a streak of melted cherry popsicle off his thumb. "Look down."

I don't have to. I know what Patrick is nodding at—the sweat highlighting what I was thinking about as it pushes against my tan work shorts. I don't respond. Instead, I bend down, reach for the test kit, flip open the lid, and pretend to double-check the chlorine level even though I know it's fine. He steps closer, stopping a few feet from the pool's edge. The sun behind him outlines his frame as he stands too close to me. Not now, please. Not today. Not in this state of arousal.

"So," he says, "big plans today?"

I shrug. "Just finishing up."

"You're usually not here this early," he notes. "Not complaining. I was getting bored."

I glance upward. "And now you're not?"

Patrick grins, lets the popsicle linger at the corner of his mouth, then bites it. "You're more entertaining than the gardener."

A soft laugh escapes as I shake my head. "You always like watching people work?"

"Depends on the view," he says. His eyes drop briefly before looking back at my face.

It's too warm out here. My chest still hums with the memory of Kevin's hands on my back, the water holding us in that electric hush. And now here's Patrick, barefoot and slick-skinned, wearing a towel and speaking in innuendo with zero hesitation. My back aches from kneeling too long, pretending to test the water while waiting for my hard-on to subside. Not sure if it's irritation or intrigue he stirs in me.

"You're not out here trying to flirt with the pool guy, are you?" I ask, keeping my tone easy.

Patrick shrugs. "What if I am?"

"I'm pretty sure you just turned eighteen."

"Nineteen, and in college."

I exhale through my nose, still crouching. "You're playing games."

He doesn't argue. He doesn't confirm it either. He stands over me with his dripping blond hair and a towel that's damper and more clingy than it should be.

"Aren't your parents home?" I ask.

"In Italy for two weeks. I'm here for two months until the fall semester."

There's a beat of silence, and then I stand. *What the hell*, I think, *let him look*. Patrick's gaze lingers. He's quieter, less cocky now. I wonder if he realizes he's not wearing his sunglasses this time—he's not hiding behind them. He's vulnerable. It's like he's waiting to see if I'll lean in or walk away.

But I don't do either. I meet Patrick's eyes and hold the look longer than needed. Not because I want to, but because part of me, the part I thought I'd buried back in that kiss with Kevin, is still humming, still awake. Desire doesn't compartmentalize just because you want it to behave that way.

"You ever go swimming?" The question changes the subject.

"Sure," Patrick says. "But I don't like cold water. I like heat. And control."

Of course he does.

"I've gotta head out soon," I say, moving toward my bag. "Got somewhere to be this afternoon."

Patrick squints at me, then tilts his head. "Hot date?"

Just long enough of a pause to let him wonder. "Something like that," I finally answer.

He doesn't move out of the way when I sling the bag over my shoulder. He stands there, his towel low around his hips, like a dare in human form. I shift past him, close enough to smell the clean scent of his body wash, like coconut and ozone, and I consider asking if I can rinse off before heading to Emory. I don't need to use the shower inside—I can strip and wash off right here, under the shady overhang of the trees on the side of the patio where guests rinse off after enjoying the pool. But I don't ask. Maybe next time.

"You should wear tan more often," he says as I reach the gate. "Looks good on you."

"Thanks," I say, "I'll keep that in mind."

The gate squeaks shut behind me. I walk to my truck, my heart beating with something I don't need or have time for. Patrick isn't what I want, but part of me still feels flattered. I can think of a hundred reasons to keep my distance. Still, none of it matters. Not when I'm heading to see Kevin.

It's just a swim. Just two old friends. Just water. Yet my hands are shaking with anticipation.

16

AFTERNOON AT EMORY

Fifteen minutes early, and it still feels like I'm running late when I walk into the Aquatic Center. The air smells like overworked air conditioning and rubber soles, humid with the warmth of bodies, filtered steam, and that faint, sour trace of damp towels and lemon disinfectant that never quite goes away. Kevin has already registered me, so I check in at the front desk with a quick release form and follow the familiar echo of water splashes, whistles, and low voices reverberating off tile and glass. Everything in here is clean, orderly, and functional. It's not a place for secrets.

Kevin appears before he spots me. He's standing near the locker room entrance in athletic shorts and a light gray Emory T-shirt that hugs the top of his arms just enough to catch my breath. His hair's still buzzed short, and he looks sharper than he did out in the courtyard at Ansley. He seems more focused now than surprised.

"Hey," he says when he sees me, smiling like this is normal. Like we do this all the time.

"Hey," I echo. My voice doesn't crack, but it's close.

We make brief eye contact—one or two seconds—then look away. He gestures toward the locker room, and we fall into step. It's quiet between us, but not tense. Just unspoken. The floor is polished and slick beneath my shoes, and every sound seems louder in the hallway. I keep my eyes ahead, careful not to stare at how the sweat darkens his shirt's collar.

"You off today?" I finally ask.

"No, I left work early. Figured I'd work out while I wait."

Inside, the locker room hums with white noise—distant showers, the occasional door squeak, and someone laughing two aisles over. We find a quiet corner to change. Kevin drops his bag onto the bench and starts to undress like it's nothing—shirt off, towel slung over one shoulder like this is just another Friday. Facing the other way, I change quickly into my swim trunks, keeping my gaze fixed on the locker doors.

When we step onto the pool deck, the light shifts—white and glaring overhead, bouncing off the water like everything's under a lens. The pool is laned, each numbered with banners that hang overhead. A few swimmers do steady laps while others stretch at the far wall. There's a pair of middle-aged men chatting near the diving blocks. The lifeguard in the corner wears mirrored sunglasses, even indoors, like he's guarding something more than safety.

Kevin nods toward lane six. "I reserved this one for us."

After rinsing at the poolside shower, we slip into the water. It's cooler than I expected, shocking my skin in a way that forces breath into my lungs. My body adjusts within seconds. Kevin dunks his head under the water, then runs his hand over his scalp as if his hair were still longer. He glides toward the far wall with a smooth, efficient breaststroke. He swims like someone who doesn't need to prove anything.

I follow, letting my limbs loosen with the rhythm of motion. The sound of the world above dulls beneath the surface, only the rush of bubbles, heartbeat, and muffled silence. I could stay down here forever. But I don't. When I surface, Kevin's waiting, his arms draped over the lane buoy, chest rising and falling easily.

Out of practice and breathless when I reach him, I say, "You look like you do this every day."

"Not as often as I'd like. "Wanna race?" he says, smirking.

I roll my eyes. "You trying to humiliate me?"

"Just trying to see if you still have it."

"Fine. One lap," I say, grinning. "Loser buys lunch next time."

Kevin shrugs. "Deal." He grabs the floating lane rope and dunks underneath it to use the empty lane beside us.

We line up, count off, and push off the wall in near-synchronicity. Kevin pulls ahead immediately—a more efficient turn and decisive kick. I let him. Partly because I'm out of practice, but mostly because I want to watch him move. He cuts through the water like a knife through silk—no wasted energy, no showing off—just speed and fluid strength.

He beats me by more than a body length. When I reach the wall, he flicks water at me. "Still cute when you try, though."

"Fuck you," I say, laughing.

We spend the next twenty minutes switching between laps and treading water at the deep end. Our voices bounce off the walls, casual and relaxed. Kevin tells me about the MBA classes he's taking. He's working at IBM, and I ask what it's like being a business analyst. Only half of it makes sense, but the sound of his voice more than compensates. I bring up a client who once asked me to turn her water pink for a bachelorette party.

He laughs, and it's real. Warm and familiar.

At one point, we drift toward the wall again. We both tread lightly, letting our arms float. Kevin leans back against the tile. His bare shoulders glisten under the overhead lights, and the pull returns—memories stirring beneath the surface like something that wants to rise.

It almost slips out: *Remember that night at your aunt's house?* Of course, he must remember. But I make no mention of it, and neither does he.

Instead, I say, "Feels weird being back in the water with you."

He glances at me. Not guarded, not open either. "Yeah. It's been a while."

I wait for him to say more, but he doesn't. He dips his head under and then pushes away from the wall. He glides backward, arms outstretched, legs sweeping in a slow, steady scissor-kick. I remain where I am, floating in the wake of his absence.

When we finally climb out of the pool, our movements are slower. I towel my face and arms, trying not to notice how Kevin's swim trunks cling to his legs. We stand side by side for a minute under the hot, humming air vents.

Kevin glances at me. "I'm glad we did this."

"Yeah. Me too."

He runs the towel over his hair once, then folds it over his shoulder. "Let's keep things simple, yeah?"

I nod. "Simple is good."

But it's not. Not for me.

We walk back to the locker room without saying much. The wet floor squeaks beneath our feet. The communal showers are visible from here, and I'm prepared to rinse off, though I'll be dripping in sweat by the time I reach my next client. A glance in his direction to take my cue, but I see he's already dried off, wearing his briefs and putting his pants back on.

He offers a quiet smile as we head toward the exit. "See you around?"

"Yeah," I say. "Definitely." It feels final enough to make me blurt out, "Hey. Thanks!"

We part ways outside the building, and there's no need to look back. I already know what Kevin looks like from behind—and that's the problem.

17

House of Contentment

(Josh)

Kevin gets home a little before five. In the kitchen, cleaning the coffee pot and loading the last of the morning's dishes, the smell of citrus soap rises from the sink. The back door opens, followed by the soft jingle of keys landing in the hallway bowl. A pause, then the creak of the laundry room door. There is a low thump, and the washer lid softly clicks shut. Then silence.

"Josh, are you home?" I hear him call from the back entrance of the house.

"In here!"

Kevin appears from the hallway a moment later, his Emory T-shirt damp and clinging to his chest. His cheeks are flush, like he just pushed through the last round of squats or sprinted the final lap.

"Damn. You smell like the gym and the pool had a baby."

He grins and walks over, leaning in to kiss me. When he steps behind and hugs me, a giggle escapes before my elbows try to bat him away.

"Stop it," I say playfully, "I'm trying to finish up here." I don't mind, really. It's nice to have a man who greets me with affection first thing when he walks through the door. When I turn to face him, a hand rests lightly on his chest for a few seconds, breathing him in. He smells like a mixture of sweat and chlorine.

"Did you swim?" I ask, even though I already know the answer.

"Yeah," he says casually. "I got off early and figured I'd work out and get a few laps in."

"The perks of having a pool at one of your two gyms," I say, half-turning back toward the sink. "And you couldn't have worn clean clothes after working out?" It's unusual for him not to shower and change after working out—it's especially true after being in the pool.

He grabs a glass from the cupboard. "Didn't pack anything extra today. I didn't know I was getting off so early," Kevin replies on his way to the refrigerator. "Besides, I was in a hurry to come home and kiss you."

I grab the dish towel to dry my hands. "Such a smooth operator. Must be that MBA training."

Kevin gives me that cocky wink and downs the water like he's been trying to swallow something all afternoon.

"You swim with one of your school buddies?"

"Nah. Just me."

His answer comes quickly and easily, smoothed out flat before I finish asking.

"Well, whatever you did, it worked. You look both pumped and relaxed," I comment, folding the towel across the oven handle.

"Yep. Needed it. Been carrying the weight of the week on my back."

"You and me both," I reply. "But hey, don't forget, we've got dinner at 7:30, remember?"

"I remember," Kevin nods. "You made the reservation."

"Baan Sookjai," I say. We've been wanting to try it for months. Roughly translated, it means House of a Happy Heart, and I like the name.

"Table by the window, just how you like," I say. "Figured we could walk—it's warm but breezy out. The fresh air will be nice."

Kevin nods again and puts his glass in the dishwasher. "Sounds good. I'm going to rinse off real quick."

"Well, you'd better do more than just rinse off," I call as he heads down the hallway.

"You can come wash my back if you want," I hear him shout from around the corner.

A smile breaks. It's a tempting offer, but I know where it will lead. There's no time now if we hope to make our reservation— an hour sooner would be a different story. We're overdue for an after-work roll in the hay, not for its romance but its sheer physicality and passion. Then again, it's Friday, and I have the whole weekend to show my man that he's hot and desirable, not just loved.

The shower hums in the background as I glance at the sorted mail. I like to sort everything into piles before opening and dealing with it. The organization helps me to sort the wheat from the chaff, as they say—the important from the trivial. And then there's the trash—the worthless inconvenience that shows up at your home uninvited and unwanted. Tackling the trash first makes focusing on the important stuff easier.

The laundry door is still ajar. As I toss in the rest of the clothes, I spot Kevin's swim trunks on top—black, brief-style Speedos, still damp and rolled tight as if he peeled them off in a rush. He never wears these to the beach. He says they make him feel too exposed. I unroll them absently, then pause. Should I fold them and put them back in his drawer when they're dry?

The lid closes with a solid click, but the thought lingers.

I'm not suspicious. Not really. Just aware. Kevin began swimming again, but he didn't mention it when he started. Still, he doesn't need my permission, and I'm glad it's helping him relax.

The thought to ask rises, but I let it fade. Kevin's always been private in small ways. He carries stress on his shoulders and keeps details close, but he's never shut me out.

We've built something solid, even if it's not flashy. We split chores without keeping score. He packs my lunch some mornings. He knows which parts of my back get tight after a rough week at the clinic, and I know how he likes his coffee. We laugh more than we fight. We listen. We try.

Still, sometimes, I feel him drift, like his thoughts are walking ahead of us, somewhere I can't follow. A reminder settles in: people are allowed to have things they don't always share. I believe in giving space, not cornering someone into explanations.

I've always been that way. I don't press. I don't pry. But that's the thing about being the patient one—sometimes, you don't realize how far someone's drifted until the space between you starts to echo.

18

Pick Up

The hostess greets me with a half-pinned updo. "Daniel Whitmire," I tell her, "for pickup."

"Yes, please," she replies, motioning me aside before turning toward the kitchen's swinging doors.

I'm dressed well enough for a pickup—black jeans, charcoal button-down, sleeves rolled to the forearms. I promised Naomi I'd grab something special, my treat, partly to make up for the friction last night. We agreed on Thai, and I'm here ten minutes early.

"Sure, thanks," I reply, relaxing to take in the atmosphere. It's a nice place, busy but comfortable, and I make a mental note to suggest we eat here next time. I glance at the patio tables behind me while I wait. How many couples? How many groups of friends? How many of those two tops are on a date?

The restaurant is busy, but it is a Friday evening. Warm lighting falls from the strings of overhead bulbs crisscrossing above the patio, casting a soft glow onto the outdoor tables. The familiar smell of ginger, lemongrass, and something slightly charred—wok-fired basil at its edge—fills the air. The place is cozy yet upscale, featuring reclaimed wood and potted orchids, with just the right amount of noise to blend the sound of individual conversations.

"Party of two—it's under Bennett," I hear behind me.

The voice stops me cold. I don't have to turn—I already know it. My heart thuds once, hard. I keep my back to him, eyes fixed on the patio through the glass. Six feet. Maybe less. I could reach out and touch the edge of the hostess stand.

I remain frozen, hoping for a few more seconds of invisibility.

"Daniel Whitmire?" one of the hostesses calls, checking the receipt stapled to the paper bags.

"That's me," I say, slowly turning to take the order from her hands.

"Enjoy."

Looking away from Kevin at first, he's now clearly visible—and unavoidable.

The blond boy stands beside Kevin as the hostess confirms their table. There are precious few seconds of unawareness when strangers are close together in crowded spaces—boarding a plane, piling into subway cars, drifting through restaurants. I take full advantage. I notice how the guy leans in when he talks, the shine on his shoes, his hair lightly gelled and combed back. How their shoulders nearly touch without trying.

Then Kevin glances up, and those precious few seconds of unawareness vanish forever.

His face shifts—not quite surprise, more like a wince softened into a smile. He looks as though he doesn't know what to say or whether to say anything at all, so I save him the choice.

"Hey, Kevin," I offer, light and casual.

The companion—Bennett apparently—turns toward me at the same time.

"Daniel?" Kevin sounds less surprised to see me than he hoped I wouldn't say his name out loud.

Bennett, who I now see is probably my age, looks at me politely but curiously. "So you two know each other?"

"Yeah, this is—Daniel," Kevin says. "He's an old friend. From Bayview."

"Oh," Josh says, engaging me with a warm handshake. "Josh Bennett. Nice to meet you."

His grip is warm. Friendly, even. I can tell from Kevin's body language and Josh's openness that Kevin hasn't mentioned me. It makes me feel protected and exposed at the same time.

"Nice to meet you," I say. The smile comes more easily than expected.

We stand there momentarily, Kevin not quite meeting my eyes while Josh studies me like he's trying to place a half-remembered name.

"From school?" Josh asks, gesturing between us.

Not even close, I think to myself.

"Ah, no. Worked together," Kevin says quickly. "And went to the same high school—hung around with some of the same guys."

Josh glances at me again. "Good old friends, then," he says with a smile. "You guys will have to catch up."

"Are you picking up?" asks Kevin. It's a clumsy pivot.

"Bennett, table for two. Right this way, please," the hostess interrupts.

"Yeah," I say, holding the bags up. "My neighbor and I are watching a movie at home."

"Sounds fun. Enjoy the movie," Josh says, stepping aside to follow the hostess. "It was great meeting you, Daniel."

He might mean it, but he also appears to want to say more. Instead, he just nods.

"You too," I reply. "I mean—enjoy your dinner. And yes, good to *finally* meet you."

Kevin nods and starts to turn before I realize what I've just said. I don't know why I say the next part. Maybe I can't just let him walk away.

"Hey, Kevin."

They both turn.

"It's a good idea. Let's catch up sometime. I'll leave my number with the hostess."

They both smile. Josh signals with a slight wave. Kevin's face flickers with something like pain behind his eyes.

As I turn to leave, I catch sight of the restaurant's name above the door.

"Baan Sookjai: House of Contentment."

Of course it is.

19

The Hunger

It starts with silence. Days pass after the dinner pick-up at Baan Sookjai, and Kevin doesn't call. The number I left at the hostess stand was Naomi's, so he now has two ways to reach me. Still, it's been five full days, and there has been no call—no casual run-ins, planned lunches, or swim sessions—just air. The silence isn't passive—it's deliberate and taut. I try not to fixate, but the absence of his call blooms in every empty moment.

By Tuesday, my apartment was spotless. The grout in my bathroom had never been whiter. Late nights pass with movies playing that barely register. During the day, I flirt harder than I mean to with strangers I don't like. Nothing sticks. Everything circles back to the same question: Was that it?

Then, Thursday morning, the phone rings. I'm still at the shop, putting some supplies in the pickup before starting my route. Everything is connected and leads back to him: cleaning supplies, pools, swimming, four years ago at night, last week at Emory—Kevin.

"Daniel! Phone call," Janice shouts through the open office door leading to the warehouse. It could be a client canceling or one with a special request. It could be what I've been waiting for. Hands wiped on my shorts, I head inside where Janice points to the second phone on the workbench. "Line two."

The room suddenly feels warmer. My chest tightens, and I pick up the receiver like it might burn.

"This is Daniel."

"Hey." It's his voice. Low, familiar, hesitant.

"Hey, you," I say back, trying not to sound like I've just come back to life.

"Sorry, it took me a few days. Things have been busy."

"It's okay," I say, "I wasn't keeping count." I absolutely was.

I glance toward the office door—Janice is still on the other line, laughing about something. The fluorescent light buzzes overhead as if it's listening.

"Did you enjoy the dinner?" I ask before the quiet has time to settle into silence. "Baan Sookjai, last Friday?"

"Yeah," he says, a soft laugh in his voice. "Josh loved it. Said it reminded him of a place he used to go to back in Bayview."

My fingers grip the edge of the workbench. "So, Josh is your boyfriend?"

"Yeah. He is."

"How long?"

"A little over two years. We've known each other for over three, though."

A silent nod, even though he can't see it. My fingers twist the phone cord. "So you were friends first?"

"Yeah."

"He seems nice," I offer.

"He is."

There's a pause. I don't want the call to end, so I reach for anything I can. "I hope I didn't say anything weird. I wasn't expecting to—well, I didn't expect any of it."

"You said finally," Kevin says, his voice dipping.

I wince. Kevin's meaning is clear, even if I pretend not to know. "Finally?"

"Yeah. You said you were glad to 'finally' meet him."

I exhale, more air than sound. "Right. That."

He lets it pass. "Anyway, I called because there's this thing tonight, a film society double feature. Josh and I had tickets, but he has mandatory PT training. It wasn't on his schedule until this week."

I don't respond. I want more context. I glance again at Janice, who's still talking to a client.

"I told him I might bring someone," Kevin adds as if that justifies everything.

"What kind of films?" I ask.

"Queer cinema. One's French and older, black and white. The other is newer, about vampires. Intimate stuff."

"So basically, sad gays making eye contact under fog."

He huffs a laugh. It's real, and it's everything. "Yeah. Pretty much."

"And you thought of me?"

"Seemed fitting."

A pause, my hand still gripping the edge of the bench.

"So, are you asking me to come with you?"

"If you're free. And if you want to."

"Yeah," I say. "I'm free."

"Great. Hey, sorry, but I've got to run. The old Plaza Theatre on Ponce; meet you there at seven."

"It's a date," I tell him.

And the rest of the day, I act like it is.

~

The Plaza glows like a dream someone else is having. I park two blocks away, and the rest I walk—better than being early and awkward. The sky's a bruised blue overhead, still holding the last streaks of summer sunlight. Still, the marquee lights have already won the color war—red neon buzzing above yellow and blue stripes like the whole building's dressed up for a premiere it hosts every night.

Letters snap into place on the signboard above the entrance: QUEER CINEMA DOUBLE FEATURE. THE HUNGER + UN CHANT D'AMOUR. One's erotic horror—David Bowie, vampires, lesbians, and gothic sensuality. The other is an old French prison flick filled with gay sex, voyeurism, and sadism. It took me nearly the whole day to get a sense of what to expect. Both promise to hurt me in entirely different ways.

There's a small crowd gathered under the building's overhang: grad students, vintage denim jackets, one guy with a chipped tooth and a copy of Interview tucked under his arm. A girl in oversized sunglasses wears a button that says, 'Love Shouldn't Have to Die in The Third Act.' Somewhere nearby, someone's smoking cloves. The scent drifts beneath the neon.

I pause just before entering the theater, beneath the hum of the signage and the low rumble of bodies. I scan the crowd, and there's no sign of Kevin.

Palms wiped on jeans, I shift forward, past the posters in glass display cases and the ticket window scribbled with showtimes in red felt-tip pen. A glimpse through the glass reveals the lobby: a worn, red carpet, gold-rimmed poster frames, and a plastic letterboard listing tonight's films as if they're part of the same heartbreak.

And then, there he is.

Kevin is already inside, near the concessions, backlit by flickering bulbs and a lobby poster for The Rocky Horror Picture Show. He looks sharp in a light blue button-down tucked neatly in slate-gray slacks, probably straight from work. He's standing with his arms crossed like he's waiting for a question he already knows the answer to.

He hasn't seen me yet, and for a second, walking feels like a forgotten skill. I stare at him through the glass. It's all so sudden— the invitation, the environment, the possibilities.

Kevin spots me and smiles, raising the hand holding our tickets. A small hand signal in return to show I see him and motion that I'm heading in.

The lobby is warm and quiet, with exposed brick walls hung with black-and-white photographs of local artists. A string quartet recording hums softly from somewhere overhead. People speak in low, reverent tones. Everyone here seems to know exactly where they belong.

"Glad you could make it," he says, extending a hand after aborting a half-hearted attempt to hug me. I do the same in return. It was awkward.

"Thanks for the invite."

The first film is beautiful in that cold, dangerous way—like touching something sharp just to feel something. It's a vampire story, but really it's about want. Hunger that doesn't stop, even when fed. There's a scene where Catherine Deneuve kisses Susan Sarandon under lamplight and silk, and it's not pornographic— it's quiet. Soft, then not. It's like love dressed up as a wound.

I shift in my seat halfway through and realize I've barely breathed. Everyone on screen is starving for something they can't say out loud. I know that feeling.

When the lights come up for intermission, I don't move. Sitting there, I try to keep the film inside me a little longer before going back out into the lobby to be a person again.

During the intermission, Kevin pours each of us a plastic cup of red wine from a linen-draped table. The crowd murmurs behind us—laughter that sounds educated, soft clinks of glasses, the gentle rustle of sports coats and scarves. Everyone here seems to have already written a dissertation on the topic of longing. One guy is wearing a T-shirt that says, 'Truffaut Ruined My Life.'

I nudge Kevin and nod toward it. "Should I know who Truffaut is?"

Kevin looks and grins, discreetly leaning in. "French New Wave director. Big on longing. Everyone's always falling in love and then falling apart. Lots of handheld camerawork and people staring out windows."

"Sounds like my kind of party."

"That's the problem," Kevin says, his smile fading. "He made it all look beautiful."

A slow nod, pretending to understand. "You bring all your almost-affairs here, or am I just special?"

I laugh too quickly—like I can disguise the fact that part of me meant it. The words hang longer than I meant them to. Kevin doesn't answer right away, and heat creeps up my neck. I suddenly wish I'd said nothing at all, but it's too late, so I smile as if I meant it as a joke.

Kevin side-eyes me and smirks, but I can tell he's not amused. "You're the only one who gets cheap wine and post-war angst," he replies.

"This feels like your world," I say.

Kevin tilts his head. "What do you mean?"

"It's cultured. Intentional. Like this version of you tonight. It's what I imagined you might become."

He looks away, smiling faintly. "And what are you tonight?"

"Lucky."

He doesn't answer, but his shoulder brushes mine. The contact is casual and practiced. But I feel it through every layer of fabric and restraint.

The second film doesn't have dialogue—just silence and breathing, smoke curling through prison bars. It's short but heavy, like a dream that won't let go. One man presses his face to the wall. Another imagines hands that never touch him back. It's not porn, but it's not subtle, either—voyeurism and repressed desire pulse through every shot—lonely, unspoken, trapped.

At one point, a prisoner blows cigarette smoke through a straw into the next cell, and I feel physical longing and the impossibility of touch in my chest.

When the credits roll, the room stays quiet. Neither of us claps. Kevin's eyes remain on the screen a few seconds longer than mine.

Outside, the patrons dissipate, and the parking lot empties quickly. A slight breeze carries the scent of moisture and summer honeysuckle. The night is warm but unsettled, as if it could storm or remain perfectly still.

We are parked near one another and cross the street together. We saunter past the Briarcliff Summit Apartments down to St. Charles, Kevin's dress shoes echoing on the old, cracked sidewalks under the streetlamps. On a quiet neighborhood corner, Kevin stops beneath a flickering bulb as the light stutters across his face.

"I keep thinking about that night," he says.

"The restaurant?"

"Bayview," he corrects. "The swim at my aunt's house. And afterward."

A swallow. Thick, heavy. "I think about it too. Not just sometimes. Always."

He meets my eyes, then lowers them. The silence between us is almost solid.

I don't reach for him. But I don't look away.

Kevin kisses me. Soft yet uncertain. His hand brushes my arm, barely there.

Then he pulls back as if it has burned.

"I shouldn't have done that."

"But you did," I say.

He exhales.

I add, quieter. "Guess we can blame the French again."

Kevin turns away, one hand gripping the back of his neck. "Josh asked about you. Last Friday night."

My stomach drops. "In what way?"

"He caught it when you said 'finally.' He waited until we got home, then asked how you knew who he was."

"So you told me this morning."

Kevin exhales. "I told him maybe you'd heard his name from someone in Bayview. But he didn't buy it."

The silence now is dense, packed tight with consequences.

"So he knows?"

Kevin shakes his head. "He suspects. There's a difference."

I nod slowly, my heart thudding. Not with guilt. Not even fear.

"Then I guess we'll find out what kind of difference it makes," I say.

Kevin looks at me. His expression is wrecked but wanting, and he remains silent.

I don't touch him again. I don't need to. Because now I know. I'm not chasing a memory anymore—and I'm not afraid of what comes next.

20

KISS OF SILENCE

The water is like glass this morning, and I hate it. It is still and unbothered. The skimmer pole slices through the surface, ripples folding over each other before settling again. I'm not even sure there's anything to scoop—a leaf or small beetle, perhaps. It doesn't matter. I need the motion. I need to feel that something's moving or changing.

The sun's already burning. My shirt clings to me in the worst places—lower back, underarms, the band where my cap meets my forehead. I don't bother adjusting it. Let it sting.

Kevin hasn't called.

Thursday night is starting to feel like a dream I keep trying to hold under my tongue, sharp at the edges and dissolving too quickly. But it's Monday now. It has been a long weekend with even longer silence. There has been no call, no word from him.

Probably busy, I tell myself. Kevin has work and classes, homework and projects, and exams to study for. He's got Josh to spend time with. Maybe he lost Naomi's number and couldn't call during the weekend. Maybe he called the shop, and I missed it. Maybe he tried, but it was the weekend. Perhaps he's not allowed to use the phone like a normal person.

But the truth presses in harder than the heat. Kevin's not calling. Not yet. Maybe not at all.

I rinse down the stone decking and check the filter. I pretend not to care. But all I can think of is the waiting, like last time, after our swim at Emory. It was five agonizing days before I heard from him, yet he eventually called. He invited me to the film festival— we laughed, we touched, and at the end of the evening, we kissed. After four years, we kissed again. And now I'm clinging to Thursday night like it meant something. Like it meant everything. Like it still might.

But what does a kiss mean when nothing follows it?

~

Naomi is sitting on the front steps of our apartment building when I park in the street in front of it. Her braids are loose, one end fraying down the side of her shoulder like she did it in a hurry. She's holding a glass of something bright and fizzy, condensation dripping down the sides.

"You look like someone spit in your cereal," she says before I'm fully out of the car.

I force a grin. "Just tired."

"Sure," she says, unconvinced. "Tired's when your eyes are puffy and you smell like shampoo. You look like you just lost a bet with God."

The car door shuts harder than I intended. "It's a Monday. Mondays suck."

Naomi hums. "Sure. But yours looks like it came with a dash of existential dread." She sips her drink, eyes still on me.

"Stop stealing big words from your clients," I say as I walk up the steps. "Speaking of which, why aren't you inside working?"

"I needed a break and some fresh air."

"So you're not out here simply to ambush me for something?"

Naomi chuckles, takes another sip of her fizzy drink, and offers it to me as I sit on the step beside her.

"Wanna hang later?" she asks. "We can watch *Tootsie* again and cry about your love life while pretending it's a comedy. Or how about *Endless Love,* and discuss your inability to process red flags?

Smirking, I wonder how long she's been sitting out here cooking up movie titles to throw at me. "My love life is fine. I'm fine," I reply.

"You're not *fine*," she says. "You're buzzing. And not in a good way."

"I'll let you know about hanging out," I say, standing to enter the building's door.

Behind me, she calls out, "That means no, which is fine. But stop pretending I can't tell the difference."

~

B-Side is quiet when I arrive, the warm light filtering through the windows casting long shadows across the bins. I head straight for the familiar shelves. Jazz first. Then Bowie. The Cars. My fingers move more than my mind does. It's not about finding anything specific. It's more about the rhythm of flipping through jacket covers, pretending that one of them might unlock the next step forward.

When Mateo arrives ten minutes later, he's still in his diner work clothes: sleeves rolled, collar open, sunglasses pushed up into the waves of his dark hair. He must have worked a double today, serving breakfast and lunch with cleanup in between. He sees me but doesn't come over to greet me, walking in like we planned to run into each other accidentally.

He heads straight for the disco and funk section and pulls out a Donna Summer album, holding it by the edge like it's a mirror. He returns it and draws out *Controversy* by Prince, giving it a little shake like he's deciding whether to commit.

"You've reorganized that section three times," he says, still not looking up.

"How do you know? You just walked in," I answer. "Besides, it was crooked."

"Nope." He finally turns to glance at me. "That's not it."

Somewhere between Nina Simone and Springsteen, I glance at Mateo's hands—long fingers flicking through sleeves with a smooth, practiced rhythm. Something is soothing about the way he moves—it's deliberate, like the albums are telling him secrets— he's reading a language he knows better than I ever will.

The first time I saw Mateo was here, maybe a year ago, not long after I arrived from Bayview. Holding a Nina Simone record, he made a witty remark about heartbreak being a seasonal disorder. I laughed, and he asked me out. A few drinks, and then sex at his place. It didn't turn into more than that, but somehow, we stayed in each other's orbit—an arrangement built on vinyl and sarcasm. There was always a quiet pull between us—something softer than friendship, steadier than desire, and easier for both of us to leave undefined.

A Rollins record gives me pause with its worn edges and yellowed liner notes. Jazz always felt like something that asked for patience. Kevin was like that—linger too long on the surface, and you'd miss what he was really trying to say.

A worn copy of The Cars' title album slips into my hand. My thumb finds the corner where the sleeve is soft and curling. Kevin loved that album. I remember us in his Bronco with the windows rolled down, heading to the beach, the Florida air full of humidity and salt. "Moving in Stereo" would come on. We'd both go quiet, pumping our heads to the deep beat and miming the words until the song rolled and melded seamlessly into "All Mixed Up," pounding our palms on the dash of his Bronco and bursting into full sing-and-shout mode.

Kevin didn't just like the same things I did—he introduced me to most of them. The Cars. The Police. George Benson. Even jazz. He once played Billie Holiday for me as if it were a confession. No one else ever did that—shared music like it meant something. At the time, I didn't get it. I thought we were just into the same bands. Now, I know better. We weren't just matching tastes; we were matching frequencies, traveling the same emotional terrain. I don't think I ever gave that enough weight.

"You look like you just saw a ghost," Mateo says, finally looking at me fully.

A soft exhale through the nose. "Kevin hasn't called."

Mateo raises an eyebrow. "Okay. So he blew you off?"

"It's not like that."

"Isn't it?"

I hesitate, then tell him anyway. "We kissed."

That stops him. He adjusts the record in his hand like he's thinking through more than just the album art. "When?"

"Thursday. He invited me to this weird little film festival at the Plaza. It wasn't even about the movie. We walked and talked a little afterward—then it just happened."

Mateo doesn't react right away. When he does, it's measured. "And now, radio silence."

I nod.

He hums. "That tracks."

"That's all you've got?" I ask.

Mateo shrugs. "What do you want—balloons? A slow clap?" He slides the Prince record back. "You don't know what it meant to him."

"And you do?"

"No," Mateo says, "but I've known enough Kevins to know how this ends. He's got a boyfriend."

I shake my head. "You don't know him."

"No," he repeats, softer this time. "But I know *you*."

The sting of it isn't in the words. It's in how casually he says them—like he's known it all along.

Mateo wanders toward the funk section again, flipping through Chaka Khan and Earth, Wind & Fire like he's cruising for a distraction. I pretend to dig into some Dylan reissues, but I'm not reading anything. Just listening to the vinyl sleeves slide against each other, that soft, papery sound that somehow feels like time passing. Kevin would know that sound. He'd name the artists I skipped. He'd care about the liner notes, the track order, and the B-side most people forget.

That's the difference. Mateo listens with detachment. Kevin listens with his heart.

We move through the shop like two people sharing the same dream from different angles. When we both reach for the same Grace Jones LP at the same time, we stop and laugh. I let him take it. He lets me pretend I don't care.

We head toward the front of the store when he asks me. "Does Naomi know yet?"

"No."

Mateo shakes his head and checks out. He leaves first, saying something about needing to go home and change before his shift at Burkhart's tonight. I tell him I'll hang back for a while, but that's not true. I don't want to leave yet, though the shop is nearly empty now. It's just me, the warm scent of old sleeves, and the creak of the wooden floor beneath my feet. It all feels like residue—something left behind.

Kevin and I used to come here. Not this exact place, but shops like it in Bayview—quiet corners filled with other people's soundtrack memories. Maybe that's what I miss most about him. Not the kiss. Not even the history. Just the way he heard things the same way I did. Like songs were messages. Like music wasn't just sound but permission to feel something all the way through. I remember that night four years ago, after our midnight swim—how he played *Zenyatta Mondatta* and *Ghost in the Machine*, low and steady in the background, like it knew something we didn't yet.

Whatever the silence means now, I'm tired of sitting in it.

Most people are now switching to cassette tapes. Some are even buying compact discs—perfect sound, no skips, no hiss, just sterile clarity. But records? They breathe. They crackle and warp and force you to sit still. You can't fast-forward a feeling. You have to let it play through in order.

Kevin is like vinyl—warm, imperfect, steady. The kind of sound you have to slow down for. And maybe that's why I keep coming back here, flipping through old pressings no one else wants. I'm not chasing what's next. I'm chasing something I didn't listen to closely enough the first time.

21

BETWEEN THE GROOVES

I run through it again in my head. I'll sit on a bench in the open-air square at Ansley Mall, just outside the bookstore across from Fitness Factory—the spot where he first saw me. A paperback in one hand, sunglasses in the other. I'll sit there, casual and nonchalant. I don't want to startle him or let him believe I'm stalking him. The goal is to see him.

It's been six days since the kiss. Six long days of silence. The kind of silence that can't be overthought and doesn't wane. Calling Kevin or dropping by the IBM building downtown was a possibility. I even considered pretending I was near Emory by coincidence, near the Aquatic Center, or even at the business school building entrance. But instead, this became the plan. For the second day in a row, I've spent my lunch hour sitting here, with a half-hour before and a half-hour after added on.

And somehow, today, it works.

Kevin appears as if summoned. This time, he's dressed in blue slacks and a white Oxford, sleeves rolled up on his forearms, carrying the same backpack I've seen before. He's sweating through his shirt like the summer heat hit him the second he left his air-conditioned office. He looks tired, as if he hasn't slept well or has been working too hard. Maybe he's hyper-focused on something. None of that matters, though. He's here.

Kevin slows when he sees me, and there's a pause between us. Then he smiles. It's not a broad smile, but it's enough. Standing with my book in hand, I say his name like I'm surprised.

"Daniel." He says it like a fact, not a question. Then, after a breath, "Hey."

There's another short pause. Kevin's eyes narrow slightly—not suspicious, just curious. "What are you doing here?"

Shrugging, I hold up the paperback and answer. "Lunch break. I figured I'd read a little. My next client's just a few streets over."

He nods slowly. "Nice spot for it."

"Yeah. Here in the shade, it's a good place to people-watch. You know me. I'm a sucker for the smell of old books and vinyl."

Kevin looks at his watch when I suggest we duck into the bookstore. "It's cooler and more private," I say. Sensing his hesitation, I promise it will only be for a minute.

We browse around the front tables as we chat, running fingers along the spines of books as we circle the displays.

"So, how's work?" he asks.

"Sweaty," I say. "Pool maintenance in the Georgia heat. You know how it is."

I catch Kevin's gaze at the paperback in my hand—*Giovanni's Room*, the one Naomi gave me nearly nine months ago, back when I pretended to be interested and told her I would read it. She said it would crack me open, not because it was about being gay but because it was about loneliness; the kind that hums under your skin no matter where you are or who you're with. I haven't made it past chapter three, though. The sentences feel too sharp, as if Baldwin knew precisely where to press. Every time I try, it's like the book is watching me. Like it already knows I'm still orbiting someone I was intimate with four years ago when I was straight and can't seem to let go.

He smiles politely but doesn't make eye contact. His fingertips linger on a new release hardcover, *The Prince of Tides*. He quickly glances at me, then slides his finger past it.

"And you?" I ask.

"Busy. Always busy."

There's a pause. Then I say lightly, "This kind of place always reminds me of you."

Kevin exhales softly through his nose. "That was a long time ago."

"Not that long," I rebut.

He doesn't argue as he circles the tables in the same manner he's circling the topic.

"Josh asked me if I was hiding something," Kevin says suddenly.

I look at him. "Last Thursday, after the films?"

He nods. "He picked up on something."

"So he knows we went together? I thought he suggested you invite me."

"Sure, he suggested it in passing," Kevin says, "but I doubt he meant it."

"What did you say?"

Kevin doesn't answer. He just looks down at the book he has just picked up from the classics table, *Invisible Man*. How fitting, I think—a novel about identity and what it means to be seen or unseen in this world.

"Did you deny it?" I ask, quieter this time.

Kevin flips the book open, then closes it, setting it back on the shelf. "It was just a moment, Daniel. Let's not make it into more than it was."

His words cut. They come from a place I didn't expect, as if it meant nothing. For a second, I freeze—part of me is afraid he's serious, that I read it all wrong—that the kiss, the silence, the way he looked at me that night was only mine. But then I see it—the way he won't meet my eyes, the way he closes the book, how his voice sounds like someone trying to control the temperature of their own heart. He's not indifferent. He's afraid. It's not the truth—it's a defense. It's a lie he needs me to believe so that he doesn't have to say more.

"Was it nothing to you?" I ask.

He doesn't reply.

I step closer to him, not enough to touch but enough to be felt. "You don't get to rewrite that night, Kevin. We both felt it."

His eyes flick to mine, then away. "I can't do this. Not now."

"Why did you kiss me, then?"

The question escapes before I can filter it. I hear the edge in my voice, too sharp and too naked. My chest tightens as the words hang between us. Shifting my weight, I'm suddenly aware of how still Kevin has gone. Part of me wants to reach for him. The other part wants to take it back. I hate that I need the answer more than I want to protect my pride.

"Because I—"

"Then have lunch with me," I blurt out before he can end the sentence, turning regret into an apology. I need more time with him: time to soften whatever has hardened, time to repair whatever has cracked, time to stop the backslide before it settles.

"I can't today," he says. "I really need to get in the gym and back to work."

The rejection lands hard, but I don't push.

"No, not today," I concede. "I need to get back, too. Sometime soon, then."

He hesitates. "Maybe."

"Good. I'll page you." I turn to leave before Kevin has a chance to give me a firm no. That's all I need.

Walking out into the bright sunlight before him, I replay the moment he said he wanted to. He's already lying to Josh—already tearing himself in half. I can see what he won't say out loud. He's slipping, and the silence between us is just another kind of music—one I refuse to let fade without hearing the whole song.

That's not the sound of rejection.

That's how fear spins—like a needle stuck between two grooves.

I can work with fear for now.

22

ECHO CHAMBER

The cicadas are screaming. It's the first thing I notice stepping into the Phillips' backyard: how the heat has squeezed their sound into this relentless electric buzz. The pool water shimmers, barely disturbed, and the air smells like sun-warmed flagstone and cut grass. Overripe hydrangeas slouch in the midday heat.

Dropping the skimmer pole beside the pool steps, I kneel to test the water. It's warm, almost too warm. It's the kind of warmth that makes everything feel dreamlike and untrustworthy. Thoughts about last Wednesday and what Kevin said in the bookstore still haunt me. He didn't say no, but neither did he say yes, which may be worse. "Maybe" is a suspended sentence—a kind of cruelty you can't prove.

The skimmer moves in slow arcs across the water's surface, like trying to smooth out a wrinkle in memory. The pool is too perfect—no leaves, no bugs—just this clear, silent mirror I can't stop stirring. The heat presses down on me, thick and slow, and hard to stop thinking about Kevin's face when he said, "Let's not make it into more than it was." That line keeps looping back like a stuck track. I try to shake it by focusing on the sound of water lapping against the tile and the low hum of the filter system.

That's when the sliding door hisses open behind me.

Patrick steps onto the upper landing, barefoot, standing just inside the line of shade cast by the awning above him. He's shirtless again—shoulders sun-warmed and golden. He's leaner and not as soft as I remembered, though he's not muscular either. His stomach is flat, his chest defined in a way that only youth can pull off effortlessly, despite being non-athletic, and thanks to privileged genes.

He's wearing another Speedo, this one navy blue with white stripes that sit low on his hips. How many pairs of swim shorts does one person need? If they are all new, is he modeling each for me each Tuesday and Friday? His dark Ray-Bans contrast with the white towel slung over one shoulder, and he's got his weight cocked on one hip as if he doesn't know—or doesn't care—what that gesture conveys.

Patrick sips from a tall, clear plastic cup. It's a reddish drink with crushed ice—maybe a strawberry daiquiri or something made to resemble one. His lips are stained red from it, soft and bright like candy. When he draws on the straw, his mouth closes slowly and deliberately, his cheeks hollowing before letting the straw fall away from his lips.

"You're sweating through that shirt," he says lazily. "Want something cold?"

I should say no to maintain my professionalism, even if it's not the kid paying for the maintenance contract. But today, I'm not interested in being professional. Today, I want to feel something sharp, something I can control.

"Sure," I say, straightening. "A soda or something. Nothing that will make my lips red."

Patrick grins and tosses back, "So glad you noticed," before turning to head back into the house. His gait is loose and confident. No, he's cocky. He knows I've already lost whatever argument I was having with myself.

He disappears into the house, towel still slung casually over one shoulder, hips moving like he knows someone's watching. There's every reason to look away—to remember this is a client's kid, barely out of high school. But something lingers. Maybe it's his inexperience, or that brazen confidence, or the way his eyes land like a dare, like the roles reversed and I'm the one hunted. Maybe there's no real attraction at all—just a question: could I have him if I wanted?

While alone, I walk to the back corner of the yard and open the pumphouse door. The equipment groans softly inside. Cramped and hot, it's like a sauna steeped in rubber and chemical residue. A low pipe forces me to duck my head as I wipe the sweat off my brow with the edge of my sleeve. The air barely stirs, and my shirt clings to my damp chest as I crouch beside the filter pump to check the pressure gauge. Even here, the cicadas buzz—muffled, but relentless.

What I don't hear is Patrick's approach. He slips inside the confined space like heat itself—quiet, invasive, impossible to ignore. Sensing movement, I turn to find him standing just behind and over me, holding a can of something cold and studying the same gauge I do. The metal can clicks against the equipment frame as he sets it down.

"Place is like a kiln," he says, his voice low and just behind my right ear.

"Yeah," I agree, clearing my throat and reaching up to adjust a valve. "Filter's running fine, though."

His breath is on my neck before I can straighten fully.

"You don't have to act like I don't know what this is," he says. His fingers skim the small of my wet back—just enough contact to be undeniable.

I remain still, half crouched and half bent over. My height and the pumphouse roof don't allow me to stand fully erect.

"This isn't a mystery, you know." His voice is softer now, almost kind. "You watch me. You linger. And maybe you tell yourself it's nothing, but you're here."

Turning, the space between us collapses until there isn't any. My back grazes the valve box as Patrick leans in, his cherry-red stained lips catching mine before fully registering the movement. It's hot, fast, open—all tongue and heat and pressure. My eyes stay open.

There's no tenderness in it—just impulse and friction.

My response is immediate—pushing back and kissing him harder. Not out of desire, but to reclaim the illusion of choice. Because Kevin kissed me and called it nothing. Because I asked him to lunch and got a maybe. Because sleep and good judgment haven't come easily in over a week.

Patrick leans back and pulls me into him, his hands clenching my wet shirt like the kind of prey that hunts through surrender, aching to be devoured and daring me to take more. And so I do.

Then I stop.

"Don't," he whispers. His lips are even redder now. "You want it."

"That's not the problem," I answer, wiping my mouth with the back of my hand.

Patrick watches me with a kind of amused disappointment. "I don't care if I'm your second choice. Just don't pretend I'm something else."

That hits hard and unexpected—the second blow of the day—and I want to react, to take it out on him. But I don't.

Instead, I step past him through the doorway, picking up the drink he brought me as I exit. The can is already sweating, cold against my palm, but I don't take a sip.

"I need to finish the pool," I say, not looking at him.

He doesn't move. "Whatever you're looking for, I hope it's worth it."

Stepping back into the sun, the air out here feels different— less like punishment and more like reality. The buzz of insects grows louder as I finish the pool in silence, every motion mechanical. Patrick has already gone into the house and doesn't come back out.

What happened in the pump house wasn't desire—it was defiance, a way to reroute the ache. Even as Patrick kissed me, there was nothing in it I wanted. Kevin hides behind his walls. Patrick offers himself. But what's missing is something neither has given, and for the first time, there's no pretending not to see it.

~

I take a long, hot shower when I get home, then put on a clean T-shirt and boxers, and collapse into bed while the sun is still setting. The sheets are tangled and damp beneath me, but it doesn't matter. I close my eyes and try to reset—try to pretend today didn't get to me.

My thoughts drift to Kevin—the way his mouth moved when he said my name. That moment in the restaurant when it almost seemed there was something still there. His shoulders, his laugh, the way he used to look at me—like I was someone he trusted, not someone he barely knew.

The images won't stay, though. Patrick bleeds in—his long torso stretched in the sun, the way he looked up at me and knew exactly what I was thinking. I try to force him out, to drag my thoughts back to Kevin, but the harder I cling to the memory, the more it shifts. Now Kevin has Patrick's mouth. Patrick's body. And I'm not sure which version I'm reacting to.

Reaching for the only kind of comfort I can summon, my fingers slide under the waistband of my briefs like muscle memory. It's desire and distraction at once—like the images of Kevin and Patrick—separate yet inseparable.

My hand moves anyway.

It's not exactly satisfying. It's more release than relief. More erasure than escape. A way to make the ache quieter for one minute, maybe two. When it's over, however, I feel worse. I've just told myself another lie and called it comfort.

I clean up, toss the shirt across the room, and pull the covers up to my chest. The ceiling fan clicks softly above me, and I stare at it long enough for the room to lose shape.

I don't know what I want anymore, just that it isn't this.

23

THIS IS LOVE, TOO

(Josh)

Our little rental house in Virginia Highlands smells like garlic and rosemary. Starting the roast a little after three, the whole place fills with the aroma. Kevin's stretched out on the sofa with the Sunday paper, but he's not reading it. A page turns every few minutes, but it's easy to see his mind is somewhere else.

Still—he's here. Not at the gym, not buried in class notes or prepping for the week. Just here, with me. We're enjoying the weather, a quiet house, and a peaceful Sunday. For now, that's enough. But even in this, there's a slight distance—he's here, but not all the way.

It's unseasonably cool today—a rare gift after weeks of heat. I've opened the windows, and the fans hum in each room, pulling in just enough breeze to make it feel like summer's finally given up. Kevin changed into cut-off sweatpants and a loose tank that slips off one shoulder. He's barefoot, his legs tan and stretched long over the armrest. I can't help but stare as I set the table.

"Dinner's almost ready," I call out.

"Are you sure you don't want help in there?" he answers from the couch.

We usually trade off—one cooks, the other cleans—but I don't need help today. He should relax, which he rarely does. I want him to know I'm here for him, that this kind of ease—the smell of roast chicken, the breeze through the curtains, me in the kitchen while he stretches out—is part of what makes us work. This is love, too—the quiet kind.

He folds the paper and sets it on the coffee table like he's been waiting for the excuse to stop pretending. He stands and stretches, then pads into the kitchen.

"Smells delicious," Kevin says, stretching again before taking his seat on one side of the small dinette table under the window in the kitchen. It overlooks the backyard, with its lush green grass and blooming hydrangeas, irises, daylilies, and butterfly bushes along the fence. This afternoon is especially nice with the windows open, the breeze gently swaying the lacy curtains next to the table that came with the house—it carries in a summery scent as if the whole yard is trying to join us for dinner.

As we eat, no television or music plays, just the quiet sounds of birds singing, trees swaying, and our conversation. It's Sunday—a time for us. We're having garlic mashed potatoes with almond green beans, fresh from the market and made from scratch, to accompany the roast. Kevin murmurs a quiet thanks after the first bite. He doesn't say much more, but he's more here now than he's been all week.

Throughout the meal, two hummingbirds dart and dash around the feeder that hangs outside the window. They compete with one another, as territorial as hummingbirds tend to be, both wanting the same thing. We usually see them from dawn until dusk throughout the day, working so hard for the same thing, as if the sweet nectar means life and death to them both. Kevin is always amazed at their skills and determination. I wish they wouldn't fight each other, but they both seem to believe it's their territory they are protecting.

I tell him a story about one of my patients—an older man who insists on calling his walker a Corvette and flirts with all the nurses. Kevin finally laughs a real laugh, not the polite kind.

"I like it when you tell me about your work," he says.

"I like it when you tell me things, too."

He nods and doesn't look away. "I know."

The rest of the dinner passes in that quiet, rhythmic pace. Kevin clears the dishes without me asking, and I let him. It feels like something small and shared. It keeps him in the present, here with me on a lazy Sunday afternoon, without any of the distractions of the outside world, and I'll take that.

"Hey, let's take a little walk to the shops. Maybe stop for an ice cream," I suggest when we finish in the kitchen. This afternoon is worth holding on to.

"Sure," Kevin agrees, "I'll put something decent on."

It's times like these when I wish we had a dog to walk with us. Kevin and I have both had dogs at different times in our lives, but not since we've been together. It's been too hectic—finishing school, relocating, and finding jobs here. It wasn't possible living in our Midtown high-rise, but now that we're here in a house with room and a yard, we'll get one soon. We just moved in, after all, and are still getting settled. I can be patient.

Home from our stroll and ice cream, we both sink into the sofa. When Kevin's head finds my lap, I run my fingers through his buzzed hair, slow and gentle, as his eyes begin to close.

"Feels so good," he whispers, speaking slowly as if he's half-asleep already. "I'm tired," he murmurs.

"Then don't move."

We stay like that past dusk after the hummingbirds stop jousting and fly back to their nests.

~

The sheets are cool when we climb into bed, the kind of sun-dried crispness that melts almost instantly beneath shared body heat. Kevin clicks off the lamp, and darkness folds over the bedroom like a soft blanket. A faint breeze from the open window stirs the curtains, letting in the sounds of distant cicadas blending with the slow churn of the ceiling fan above us.

I turn toward him, and for a second, we breathe in silence. The house is quiet, with only the settling creaks of an old floorboard and the gentle hum of summer night air.

"Do you want me to run us a bath?" I ask quietly, reaching for his hand. "We could soak and relax."

Kevin's fingers squeeze mine, and he smiles, but it's faint in the dark. "That sounds nice," he says, brushing his thumb over my knuckles. "But we're already in bed, and I think I'd fall asleep in there."

"Another time then."

He brings my hand up to his lips and kisses it—just a brief, warm press—and rolls onto his side to face me.

His hand finds my chest first, fingers spreading gently over my sternum like he's checking to see if I'm real. Then he touches my face, a featherlight graze across my cheek, before leaning in to kiss me. The kiss is slow and intentional. It's not hungry. It's not rushed. It's careful. Present.

My hands move to his back, smooth and warm under my palms, then down to the curve of his waist. He exhales softly, the sound catching between us, and I feel the tension start to leave his body. When he climbs over me, knees bracketing my hips, I welcome the weight, the closeness. I want to be wanted. I want him to feel wanted.

He kisses my neck and chest. We still don't speak. It's not silent, though—not with the sound of his breath, the shift of skin on cotton sheets, the low thrum of the fan mixing with the occasional rustle of night sounds outside.

Kevin's body feels familiar and new all at once—like a song I forgot I loved until the melody starts playing again. My hands trace his back, grounding myself in him. When I whisper his name, he looks into my eyes. They shimmer in the faint moonlight streaming through the window. There's something raw in them, a glassiness or need. Then he kisses me again, deeper this time. A kiss that feels urgent.

The rhythm changes—more urgency, more need. Kevin's grip tightens, and I feel his breath warm against my skin with a kind of desperation that catches me off guard. His stubble burns lightly along my collarbone as he moves lower. I feel the warmth of his breath, the press of his lips, his hands skimming down my ribs, then digging into my thighs.

My fingers trace the taut curve of his shoulder blades and the slick heat of his lower back, marveling at how alive he feels—like a live wire drawn tight and finally allowed to spark. His hips press against mine, and we move together, clumsy at first, then caught in the rhythm. Kevin's skin is hot and flushed, and his breath is ragged and fast.

I'm overwhelmed. Not just by surprise and sensation, but by Kevin's want and passion—the way he moves, like he needs this to mean something. It's like he's pouring himself into me to keep from falling apart, and I'm the only place left where he feels whole.

We move together, as if we've done this a hundred times, yet we're relearning it all at once. He's more intense than usual—not just present, but ravenous in the way he touches me, the way he grips my hips, the way he drives into every motion like it's the only way he can say something he doesn't have words for.

I open myself to Kevin and let him take whatever he needs, and for a while, stop wondering what he's not saying. His breath mixes with mine until I can't tell where one ends and the other begins. Whatever this is, whatever brought it on, I want it. I want to be what he turns to when everything else feels too much.

He shifts closer, the movement seamless, as if it were instinct, like something raw and primitive. He holds my legs as we move together, the rhythm building between us. The moonlight slicing through the window catches Kevin's eyes, casting silver across his cheekbones and collarbone. His jaw tightens, eyes locked on mine—he looks wild and heartbreakingly powerful, like someone chasing something he doesn't understand yet doesn't want to lose again. His breath stutters with each push, each motion, like he's trying to drive some truth deeper than words ever could.

I grip his forearms as his motion grows intense, until everything gives way to something quiet and spent, like surrender.

He eases back into my arms with a quiet gasp, breath shaky, chest heaving as we fall into stillness. I wrap an arm around him and pull him tight against me, as if it were possible to be any closer, any more complete, any more in love.

His head comes to rest on my chest, skin flushed and damp. My fingers drift through the buzzed hair at the nape of his neck, slow, grounding strokes.

"You okay?" I ask, just above a whisper.

He nods, lips brushing against my chest. "Yeah."

And for tonight, I believe him.

His hand settles on my stomach, tracing slow, absent-minded circles. His breathing begins to even out.

But I'm still awake.

The fan casts slow-moving shadows across the plaster as the heat cools between us. The silence settles in again, and I wonder about the way he moved tonight—about the edge in it—the hunger that didn't quite match the gentleness we usually share. It felt like something being released—like he had held his breath for days and finally let it out all at once.

I'm not unhappy. Not at all. If anything, it felt like I reached Kevin—like I gave him something he needed. But still, part of me wonders. Part of me says it didn't feel like Kevin. Not the way I know him. Not entirely.

As his body falls into relaxation, the sounds of the distant cicadas return to our bedroom, lulling him to sleep. He stirs slightly, then settles again.

It wasn't soft—not in the usual way. But maybe this is love, too, the kind that rushes in when words won't come. Whatever truths he hasn't told, I have this moment, this closeness, and I hold onto it like it's enough.

24

RED BEANS AND RECKONING

Naomi's apartment smells like ginger and cardamom when she answers her door barefoot, wiping her hands on a kitchen towel. Dinner is simmering on the stove, and incense curls from a dish on the windowsill. Mismatched pillows spill across the couch, and dim amber light glows from a lamp with a beaded fringe. Naomi always knows how to make a space feel like it gives a damn.

"You're late," she greets me.

"You said *around* six," I reply.

She raises an eyebrow. "Get in here, boy," she says, swiping my behind with the dish towel as I enter.

Mateo is slouched in the corner of the couch, arms folded, giving me a look as if I arrived late on purpose to endure Naomi's commentary on whatever social fire she's decided to put out tonight alone.

"Look who showed," he says. "Thought maybe you got swept away by your noble quest for closure."

"Traffic," I respond, shooting him a glance and an insincere smile.

"Traffic from 2B? Bullshit."

Naomi returns from the kitchen with three glasses of a deep brown liquid. She hands me one.

I take a sip of the small but potent cocktail. "Damn, girl. We're drinking straight bourbon now?"

"Boy disappears for a week and acts surprised we restocked the good stuff," she says, speaking to Mateo but nodding in my direction as she settles into the armchair with her glass.

"So let's go around the room. How was work, Daniel?"

"Fine."

"You seem off," she says, casually but not. "Actually, you've been off for weeks."

Mateo doesn't wait to comment. "He's not off. He's spiraling."

Naomi leans forward, studying me. "I haven't heard a single late-night shenanigan from your apartment in a while. I haven't heard you bringing in or taking out any of that trash."

"Haven't seen you at Burkhart's either, since when, that night you blew off dinner at the Colonnade with Naomi?" Mateo adds.

"I've been lying low," I tell them, "staying out of trouble."

"That's not like you," Naomi says. "You disappear when you're being bad, not when you're good."

There's a silence, and then Naomi lifts her glass. "Well, whatever's going on, I'm still glad we're here. Good friends are hard to find. Cheers."

Mateo clinks his glass to hers. "And harder to keep if you lie to them."

I raise mine reluctantly. "To good friends."

Naomi sips. "Now. About what's been keeping you in hiding."

"I've just been busy. That's all."

"Doing what?" Mateo asks. "Watching Kevin from the bushes?"

My drink freezes halfway to my lips. I shoot Mateo a look, but he doesn't flinch. It's the third time he's brought up Kevin in front of Naomi—like he's daring me to say it out loud. I can't tell if he's annoyed, trying to be funny, or just trying to crack the silence open enough for the truth to fall out.

Naomi's voice is quieter. "Are you stalking that boy?"

"Dinner smells great, by the way. What are we having?" I ask.

"Red beans and rice with andouille sausage, and you didn't answer my question," she says.

I tell myself it'll sound different out loud—that once I say it, maybe they'll finally get why I keep showing up for someone who told me not to.

I exhale and glance at Naomi. "We went swimming two weeks ago, a couple of days after I used your phone. He kissed me. Now he says we should forget it. Okay?"

Mateo straightens. "You told me a week ago that you guys went to the movies. You didn't mention swimming together. What else has happened that you haven't mentioned?"

"A week ago?" Naomi shouts. "And you haven't said shit to me?"

I take another gulp from the glass, and it burns all the way down.

"He invited me to swim at Emory, and I went. That night, I ran into him and his boyfriend at the Thai place when I was picking up our order. Then he invited me to see a double feature the week before last. That's when he kissed me."

Naomi shifts forward in her chair. "You met his boyfriend and the next week were kissing each other at the movies?"

Mateo stares at me. "That's not what you said at the record shop. You skipped the swim. You skipped the restaurant. You skipped the boyfriend."

"I didn't skip it. I just didn't think it mattered." I saw no point in mentioning the lunch we shared or our phone calls.

"It matters," Naomi says. "You know he has a boyfriend, yet you guys are going swimming and to the movies and kissing? What else aren't you telling us?"

"We're not doing anything anymore. Kevin told me to forget it. To forget it all."

Mateo frowns. "He told you that when?"

"Last Wednesday. I saw him at Ansley. I waited for him outside his gym at lunchtime."

"You waited?" Naomi repeats. "Why haven't you told us any of this?"

"It doesn't matter now," I tell them. "He told me the kiss was nothing, not to make it more than it was."

"What an asshole," Naomi remarks.

Mateo stands and paces. "Jesus, Daniel. That's not reconnecting with an old friend. That's chasing someone already in a relationship."

"I know what it looks like."

"Do you? Because from here, it looks like an obsession."

Naomi doesn't speak right away. When she does, she does it carefully. "This isn't about Kevin. You said you were trying to figure things out, but you're not. You're trying to make a moment from four years ago come back to life."

"You don't know what happened."

"Of course we don't," she says. "So why don't you enlighten us?"

I look down. My glass is empty.

"We were friends. We hung out together and worked at the same place. He moved away, I got married, and then we ran into each other one night a couple of years later when he moved back."

"Yeah, and?" Naomi presses.

"And—we had sex one night. Well, kind of. Kevin was my first, but I didn't handle it well, I guess. I kinda freaked out and ran out on him. That was four years ago—before I came out and burned everything down."

"And here you both are living in the big 'ol gay city of Atlanta," Mateo says.

For a moment, no one speaks until Naomi stands and takes my glass to refill it. "We're not your audience, Daniel. We're your friends, so stop performing and tell us what the hell you're doing with this guy."

Trying to think of something to say, I tell myself that if I can find that thread again between Kevin and me, maybe I can undo the damage between us. The trouble is, I'm the only one who sees the damage. I'm the only one in the room who feels the scars. Kevin must feel them, too. He must. I don't say any of it, though. I take the refilled glass from Naomi's hand and sit back down.

"Dinner's ready," she calls from the kitchen, her voice more relaxed and distant now. She heads to the table and starts dishing out red beans and rice.

Neither Mateo nor I move right away. The air is too congested with everything said—and a few things unsaid. Then he breaks first, standing and stretching like it's just another Monday.

"Come on," he says. "If we're gonna judge you, might as well do it over food."

The bourbon still burns in my chest, but the silence burns deeper. The table feels larger tonight, as if the three of us share a room but not the same moment.

Naomi glances at Mateo, and for a second, no one moves. We're still in the wreckage of our words, but the rice is ready. And so, we eat.

After dinner, Naomi puts on a record—something low and bluesy. Mateo clears the dishes without being asked. I stay seated, staring at the bottom of my glass like it might hold an answer.

Naomi finally breaks the quiet. "Dessert is in the fridge if either of you wants it."

I stand and shake my head. "I should go."

"You always say that right before you disappear for days," she says.

"I won't disappear." That's a lie.

Mateo watches me move toward the door. "You keep chasing the past like it owes you something. It doesn't, mi amigo."

Naomi's voice follows, low and firm. "You think this ends with Kevin loving you. But it ends with you hollowed out and alone."

Opening the door and stepping into the hallway, the music plays on behind me. The smell of red beans and rice still lingers. I walk into 2B, but part of me is still at that table—sitting in the silence, waiting for affirmation that I'm not crazy or self-destructive for wanting Kevin. It won't come from them, however, so I close the door behind me.

It doesn't feel closed. Not really.

25

ALMOST HONEST

(Josh)

The kitchen is quiet except for the hum of the refrigerator and the ticking of the wall clock. I've just finished wiping down the counter, rinsing the last pan, and stacking the dry plates. Kevin's in the living room, sitting sideways on the couch with a book in his lap. I haven't heard a page turn in ten minutes.

I dry my hands on the towel and lean against the sink. Kevin's got a copy of *The Stranger* in his hands—creased spine, pages soft from too many starts and stops. He's been trying to finish it since before we moved here. I lent it to him after we met, back when things were easier—when he still had time to read for pleasure, not just for class.

"You're quiet tonight."

Kevin doesn't look up. "Just tired."

I nod, but I don't buy it. The air between us is already doing the talking. "That film night we had tickets to. You said you might invite someone."

His fingers become tense around the book. "Yeah?"

"You didn't mention much about it afterward. Did you go with anyone?" I watch him lower the book and peer out the window into the backyard as if he's trying to remember what happened two weeks ago.

I save him the trouble. "Was it Daniel?"

There's another long pause. "Yeah."

"Why didn't you tell me you took him?" I ask, setting my glass down on the table.

"It wasn't a big deal, and I haven't thought much of it since. Besides, you never asked." Kevin finally puts the book down and looks at me. He remains seated. The great divide between the kitchen and the living room still separates us.

"That night you bumped into him at Baan Sookjai—when you introduced me—that wasn't the first time you guys reconnected, was it?" He looks like a deer in headlights on a dark Southern road in the dead of night. He doesn't have to answer.

"I knew it," I say. "I knew it when that boy told me he was glad to 'finally' meet me. What a peculiar thing to say, don't you think?"

"It's not like that," he says.

"Then what is it like? Explain it to me."

Kevin's shoulders rise and fall with each careful breath. "He's from my life before. He reminds me of who I was—when things were different."

"Different how? When you were confused and fresh out of a straight relationship with a woman? Is that the 'you' he reminds you of?"

"No, of course not," Kevin replies.

"Is this the boy you told me about? That first day, when we spent hours talking at the diner, the friend you had sex with for the first time? The one who ran out on you? Are we talking about *that* Daniel?"

The pieces are falling into place.

"Yeah," he says, "that was him. But that was a one-time thing a long time ago."

"So that has nothing to do with now?"

Kevin falls silent for a moment. "I didn't say that."

His answer isn't no. But it isn't yes, either. And suddenly, I'm back in my childhood kitchen in Bayview, the year my father moved out.

~

It's summer, and I'm nine. The light through the blinds stripes the counter, and the air smells like coffee and fried eggs.

Mom's washing dishes, her shoulders set. Dad stands near the pantry with his hands in his pockets, not looking at her. I can't hear what started it, only what's left. He says, "You're making it bigger than it was." And she says, "Then why won't you say it didn't happen?"

There's no yelling. Just the sound of water running too long and the hollow clinking of plates. I'm frozen, sitting on the floor in the hallway, hidden by the wall, clutching a Matchbox car in my fist like it might anchor me. Even now, I can hear her voice—quiet but cutting. "You think I need proof? I don't need proof. I can feel when something's gone." That house never felt smaller.

He didn't confess. He didn't apologize. He just walked out of the room, like silence was enough.

Two weeks later, he was gone for good.

That's what I think of when Kevin won't answer. That feeling of being handed silence and told it should be enough. It never is.

I move around the kitchen island, not to close the gap, but to remind myself there is one. "So, you saw him before *and* after I met him—when the two of you pretended you hadn't seen each other in years?"

Kevin nods. "Yeah."

"Where?"

"We had lunch. Just once. We ran into each other at Ansley, outside the gym."

"Just lunch?" I breathe deeply through my nose, steady. "Anything else?"

He shakes his head, but the response feels too quick. "No. Not really. We've just run into each other a couple of times and chatted briefly. That's it."

"Chatted about what?"

Kevin's voice drops. "The past. What's happening now. Work. Us. It's nothing."

He stands, but the space between us doesn't close.

"About us? I don't need you talking to an old fuck buddy about us."

I don't even care what was said. What stings is the silence—how many things Kevin has told Daniel that he didn't think I could handle or didn't care to share with me.

I fix my gaze on him—the way his arms are folded and pulled tight across his chest like he's bracing for impact.

"You talk about the past like it's some safe little memory," I say. "But if it were, you wouldn't be this shaken. So what is it? Guilt? Regret? Or are you hoping for something?"

Kevin opens his mouth, then closes it. His hands tighten into fists at his sides.

"I don't know," he finally says. "I don't know what I want."

"Have you two had sex?" I ask.

"Of course not."

I believe him. But that's not the point. Not even close.

"That's not the betrayal," I say.

Kevin's eyes search mine like he's waiting for the axe to fall. "Then what is?"

"Not telling me about him. Not talking to me about it."

He looks away, and I can see his eyes begin to well up with tears. The silence that follows isn't heavy—it's hollow, like a vacancy. Like love and trust have already left the room.

"I just want to know what's true," I say quietly, "before it becomes something else."

Kevin maintains his gaze out the window, away from my eyes. "I didn't mean for this to happen."

That's what my father said once, too, as if intention could erase impact, or being sorry was the same thing as being honest. And just like back then, I'm the one left trying to read the silence and pretend it counts as closure.

"I know." At the sink, I pour out the rest of my drink. The silence behind me stays still, like it's watching. "But it did."

No reply comes. Without a word, I step out of the kitchen— no slamming doors, no raised voices. Left with his silence and my disappointment, the rift is no longer invisible. There's no going back now.

From the hallway, I see him lean forward and reach for the phone. His hand hovers there, just inches from it. Then he pulls back. A moment passes, and he crosses the room and walks out the back door. The late afternoon breeze hits him, calm, quiet, undeserved. He steps outside without looking back.

I can see Kevin from the window in the bedroom. He's sitting on the back deck, lit only by the spill of amber light from the kitchen as the sun sets. His shoulders are slumped forward, his hands folded between his knees.

I watch him for a moment. I don't feel angry—just distant. It's like looking at someone trying to remember who they are, and I can't help but wonder if he's thinking about Daniel. Was he thinking about Daniel the last time we made love? He was hungry, ravenous, almost desperate—like he needed to erase something. I felt it then—the difference—but I didn't say anything.

Now I wonder when he began to drift—how many times, even in our most intimate moments, he was already somewhere else, already thinking about Daniel.

Maybe he's waiting for things to mend themselves—or to finally break. All I know is, I can't keep hoping honesty will walk in on its own.

26

A POLITE WARNING

The long holiday weekend drags like an empty threat. I spend most of it alone, pretending to need the rest. Invitations to picnics and fireworks go unanswered, replaced by the background noise of the TV on low volume. I tell myself I'm recharging—but really, I'm waiting for a call that never comes. Kevin is probably with Josh at Piedmont Park or grilling hamburgers with their friends, waving sparklers and smiling like nothing's amiss. It's not jealousy. It's the ache of being dismissed before I even got the chance to matter.

By Sunday, I'm beyond hurt, debating whether to wait him out or force his hand, rehearsing what I might say, running through conversations we haven't had yet. The silence is saying enough—but if he won't answer it, maybe I will. I don't want to ruin anything, but I also don't want to be forgotten—if I have to cause a little discomfort for him, so be it.

By Monday, I'm glad to be out of my apartment and back to work. It means being around people again, although I've avoided them all weekend. I couldn't face the festivities, the celebrations, the happiness of people enjoying their time together, while I had no one.

Morning haze hangs low over the cracked pavement behind the shop. I'm half-listening to the local FM station crackling from the radio inside while I reload the pickup with clean skimmers and fresh chlorine tablets. It's easier to focus on what I'll do next if I'm already doing something now.

The truck is loaded when the metal door between the office and the warehouse creaks open. It's Janice, holding a cordless phone in one hand and a cigarette in the other.

"Daniel," she calls, squinting. "Phone's for you. He asked for you by name. Sounds like that guy again."

Wiping my palms on my shorts, I take the phone, my pulse kicking faster. It's got to be Kevin. Maybe he changed his mind. Perhaps the silence over the weekend meant something to him, too. He's probably calling to grab lunch again or meet up to swim. If he's reaching out, then maybe there's no need to be so hard on him. All that rehearsing—what to say, how to keep my distance— suddenly feels like weekend noise, just a shield I might not need.

Lifting the phone to my ear, I feel my heart in freefall. "This is Daniel."

"Daniel. Hey, it's Josh. Josh Bennett."

I freeze, caught between the sound of his voice and the sudden drop in my chest. It's not Kevin. It's never Kevin when I want it to be. For a second, all the rehearsed charm, the effortless cool I've been building like armor, vanishes.

"I don't mean to interrupt your day," he says. "I was just calling to hear the voice that's been echoing through my house lately."

A few seconds pass without saying anything. Josh's statement stuns me, and I can hear my heart pounding in my ears.

"Josh. Uh—everything okay?"

"Everything's fine," he says calmly. "Thought I'd say hi, that's all."

"Okay."

There's another pause. I listen for sounds in the background but hear none. Josh must be at work by now—or maybe he's at home. I wonder if Kevin is there with him.

"Just one question," he says. "You and Kevin—when did you reconnect? How long has this been going on?"

Josh's tone is calm. Mine is coming undone. My heart pounds, tight and fast, as if it wants to burst out. "A few weeks ago. Maybe a month. When we ran into one another, that is. But there's nothing—"

"Just curious," he interrupts. "I like to know what kind of energy is entering my life."

A new silence hangs between us. It's uncomfortable and unnerving, at least for me, and I try to assess my options as quickly as my mind can control my emotions. I've rehearsed the call all weekend, but that was for Kevin, not for Josh.

I try a small, deflecting laugh. "Is that what this is?"

"I don't think it's a mystery anymore, Daniel. I just wanted you to know. I see you."

I don't have time to respond before the full weight of it hits me. Josh is not calling to question anything. He's calling to end the illusion that this is a secret—that Kevin is just confused—that I'm operating in the shadows. He's telling me the lights are on, and I've been center stage the whole time.

And just like that, I feel bare, not guilty necessarily, and not exposed in the way Kevin makes me think I should be. This is different. Strategic. Like being marked.

Josh's voice softens, but it doesn't let go. "Have a good day, Daniel."

Then, the line clicks.

I stand with the phone to my ear for a few seconds. Janice is already back inside. The radio hums some second-rate power ballad from last year. I place the handset on the shop bench gently, as if I were holding something fragile that I don't know how to handle.

The rest of the day moves around me, but I'm somewhere else. Every word from that call plays back in my head, one line at a time. I don't call Kevin. I don't say a word to anyone.

Because now I know. Josh isn't wondering anymore. He's watching, and the dynamics of the game have just changed.

27

LINES WE CROSS

Half-expecting to see Patrick at the Phillips pool, I find the chair by the shallow end empty. He probably spent the long weekend up at Lake Lanier with other college brats. Just as well—his swagger, slow-burn confidence, and flirtation aren't something I'm in the mood for. There's no time anyway, not with the appointments I'm still making up from last Friday.

The next job is off Scott Boulevard: an old bungalow with a cracked stone patio and a kidney-shaped pool that hasn't seen swimmers all summer. The house is empty; the clients have already moved out of town. It's going on the market soon, which honestly suits me. No nosey clients. No entitled teens. Just time to think.

Josh's voice still lingers—cool, polite, surgical—like he was confirming a diagnosis he already knew. And Kevin still hasn't returned a page. Three sent on Monday. Another three today. I've heard nothing. I may send a few in the evenings if he doesn't start responding.

I'm not mad. Not yet. But the silence is creeping in, heavy and thick like the air before a storm. I know the signs. I've lived in this kind of waiting before—where silence is just another way of saying no.

My skin's already tingling from too much sun. I pull the hose and brush out of the water to rinse them off. Sitting at the edge, feet in the water and arms draped over my knees, I watch the shimmer of light ripple across the surface like a memory. For a second, I'm fifteen again—standing stiffly in a cheap suit and sweating through my dad's cologne.

~

Amy Carlton was the first girl I asked out. I was fifteen, and that was what I was supposed to do at fifteen. She was sweet, always smiling at my jokes. We went to the homecoming dance together. She wore a green dress with sequins and smelled like hairspray. I remember our slow dance most—how awkward my hands felt on her hips, how I avoided looking at her lips too long.

After the dance, I walked her to her door. She kissed me on the cheek and said, "I thought you were gonna kiss me for real." I smiled, said something dumb like, "Next time," and walked home alone, palms sweating and heart racing for reasons I didn't understand.

There wasn't a next time. Amy avoided me for a week and then told her friends I was weird. She said I wasn't interested in girls like that. Looking back, I guess she was right. Maybe I already knew and just wasn't ready to face it.

~

Now I'm here again. Watching something I don't quite understand slip away before I have a chance to call it mine. I didn't know what I wanted back then, but I do now, and it's not Amy. It's Kevin. And I can feel him pulling away before I've had the chance to hold onto him.

Leaning back on my elbows, I let the sun hit my face and close my eyes. If he stays silent today, I'll page him again tomorrow. He may think he can pull away quietly, but I'm not disappearing, not this time, not without being seen.

~

It's Wednesday, the third day I've been paging Kevin since Josh's call. I paged again this morning, just after arriving at the shop. No response. Not a single call returned—just silence, thick as ever, stretching wider by the hour.

I remind myself he's busy. That Josh is watching him closely now. That Kevin's guilt has him frozen, or Josh's threats have him handcuffed. But none of it makes the waiting feel any less ignored or, worse, erased.

At the warehouse, deliveries arrive steadily, and the shelves need restocking. Every time the phone rings, I pause—only to find the call isn't for me. Until one is.

"Daniel, line one!" Janice calls out. "When are you gonna get a fucking phone at home?"

"When this place pays me more money," I shout back.

I don't move at first. I wipe my hands on a towel and reach for the extension hanging above the shop's workbench.

"This is Daniel."

There's a pause. "Hey, it's me."

My throat tightens. It's anger that swells within me first. Still, I remember anger won't get me what I want, so I take a deep breath to keep the irritation, relief, and desire interwoven within me measured.

"Took you long enough," I say flatly. I want to yell, to punish Kevin for the silence—but I bite it back. Losing control now means losing him forever.

"I know," he says. His voice is low, and he sounds rushed or stressed. "I'm sorry. I—I didn't know what to say."

"Try starting with why Josh called me."

Kevin doesn't answer right away. "Josh called you? Jesus Christ. When?"

"Monday morning." I pause. "Don't tell me you had nothing to do with that."

"I swear I didn't," Kevin says quickly. "What did he say?"

"He said I've been echoing through his house or some shit like that. He asked me how long 'this' has been going on."

I could hear Kevin exhaling hard, like punched in the gut. I can almost picture him slumped over whatever desk he's calling from, his hand pressed to his forehead.

"I didn't think he'd actually—"

"You didn't think at all," I snap. "You lit the match and vanished."

"I'm sorry, Daniel."

"No, you're scared. Do you know Josh told me he just wanted me to know that he *sees me*? What the fuck is that supposed to mean?"

Another silence. This one feels like a retreat.

"I didn't mean for this to happen," he says.

"Then meet me. Tomorrow at lunch. Talk to me like a person, not a mistake."

"I can't. Not now. I need to fix things with Josh."

"You invited me back in, Kevin. You had lunch with me. You asked to see me again, invited me to swim, and took me to the movies. You kissed me, Kevin. You said you remembered."

"I do remember." His voice cracks on the word.

"Then don't act like we imagined this. One lunch. One hour. Or I swear I'll knock on your front door, and all three of us can have this conversation."

I can hear Kevin swallow.

"Ansley. Friday at Noon. I have an all-day workshop tomorrow and won't be able to meet. Does that work?"

"Yeah. I'll be there."

He hangs up first without a goodbye—just the dead click of something unresolved.

I replace the receiver slowly, my hand still trembling.

Kevin agreed to meet, but the hesitation clung to every pause, every sigh. The call drained me. Being sharp—pushing—was necessary, but it's not what I want. Not really. I don't want to corner him. I want him to want me. To choose me. Not because he's scared of what Josh or I will do, but because he still feels what I know is there.

I didn't fight for lunch. I fought for a chance. And now I'm back where I started—waiting in silence, hoping it means he's thinking. Dreading it means he's gone.

28

THE ROMANCE OF MISERY

I arrived at Ansley thirty minutes early, thanks to lighter-than-expected traffic and rushing through my first two appointments. A shady table near the far end of the square offers the best view of the parking lot, the same table where Kevin and I first spoke. It's half past eleven, so the lunch crowd hasn't hit yet. A waitress brings water without asking, assuming I'll be eating at this café. I thank her, then check my watch.

Kevin said Noon.

The ice cube lingers against my lips as I sip the water slowly. I'm sweating through my shirt already. The traffic on Piedmont is sluggish, a string of brake lights blinking at intervals. I count the red cars. Four. Then six. Then seven.

My watch draws my eye—11:37, 11:43, 11:52. Every time I tell myself to stop, my eyes drift back anyway. People trickle in and out of the café—some in gym clothes with towels slung over their shoulders, others dressed for lunch dates or business meetings. A man jogs by with his shirt off, sweat trailing down his back like rainfall down a wall.

I study each new arrival in the parking lot, guessing who might be Kevin. I don't even know what he drives. Will he walk up from the gym entrance or come from the lot? Will he be in work clothes or already dressed for the gym? I picture it again and again, rehearsing my face when I see him. Do I smile? Stay cool? Stand? Stay seated? Each possibility sifts through my mind like sand.

Time moves in slow, deliberate ticks. Why can't he be early, just this once?

Noon comes and goes.

The chair shifts beneath me. Arms cross, then uncross. A glance around—cool, casual, unbothered—like I'm waiting on a friend, but my leg won't stop bouncing.

The sun shifts, and the line of shade is moving past me. I ask the waitress to move to another table. She's kind and lets me switch. I scan the lot again.

12:09.

Kevin is late. Maybe he's stuck in traffic. Perhaps a meeting ran long. It could be he's on his way right now, rehearsing what he'll say, just like I did. I wonder if Josh knows about this—if Kevin told him. If he's being watched. If he's afraid.

12:14.

I order a Coke to keep the waitress from checking on me again. When it comes, the ice is already melting. I take one sip, then push the glass aside. If Josh knows, maybe he said something. Maybe Kevin didn't forget—perhaps Josh told him not to come.

- 12:19.

Our last call replays—every pause, every sigh, the way Kevin's voice cracked when he said, *I remember*. I wish I didn't.

Maybe he's parking. Maybe he's already walking up, and I just haven't seen him yet. One more minute, I tell myself. Just give it one more minute.

12:26.

I glance at the empty chair across from me. For a second, I imagine Kevin in it—arms crossed, lips parted like he's about to apologize or explain or lie. The water glass slides an inch toward the empty seat before the realization sets in.

12:31.

He's not coming. I feel it now—not like a thought, but like gravity. No footsteps. No shadow falling across the table. No second chance walking up from the lot.

No one's coming.

My jaw tightens as cash lands on the table—careless now. Nothing is worth finishing. I don't bother to refold the napkin. I leave it crumpled, like the hour just wasted.

By the time I reach the Phillips' property, I'm done pretending to feel anything but pissed.

~

For once, Patrick isn't draped across the lounger by the shallow end. Perhaps he's still away, or maybe his parents have returned from Italy. Then the movement by the back stairs catches my eye. It's Patrick, and he's just coming out of the house barefoot and dressed like he has plans to be somewhere else in white linen shorts and a blue polo shirt.

Patrick stops when he sees me. "Oh boy," he says, eyebrows raised. His Ray-Bans sit on top of his head, which he lowers to shade his eyes. "You've got that look again."

"What look is that?"

"The look people get when they're in love with someone they shouldn't be," he says.

"Not in the mood today, sonny," I say.

"You're never in the mood, pool guy," he quips back.

I chuckle, but not from humor. It's more about acknowledging that I'm the paid service provider, and his parents are the clients who are paying. "What do you know about love?"

Patrick shrugs and sits on the edge of the pool, dipping his feet into the water. "I know enough to see what it does to people. It makes them brave sometimes, but it also makes them stupid a lot of the time. Makes them miserable most of the time and horny the rest."

How astute for a nineteen-year-old prick, I think. The skimmer gets checked, then the brush meets the tile. "Sounds about right."

"The worst part," he says, watching the ripple trail from his toes, "is it tricks you into thinking misery's romantic. Like if it hurts enough, it must be real."

Something about how he says it—unpolished but honest—slows me down. The brush rests against the tile as I half-turn toward him.

"You've been hurt?" I ask.

He shrugs again—no smirk this time, just something quieter beneath it. "Haven't you?"

For a moment, we sit in it—the heat, the hush, the things neither of us is saying—while the cicadas keep buzzing like they know something we don't.

Then he kicks water at me.

"What the hell—"

"You need to cool off," he grins.

A playful lunge sends him stumbling back, laughing. I give chase and catch him, and soon, we're grappling by the pool's edge, trying to grab each other's wrists while slapping one another's hands away—until I fake him out and tug hard enough on him to launch us both into the pool.

The splash is enormous, and water floods my nose. I surface, sputtering, and slick my hair from my face. Patrick comes up beside me, spitting water in my face and laughing uncontrollably.

"You're a bastard," he says.

"You're not wrong."

We drift to the wall, holding onto the edge.

Patrick retrieves his sunglasses from the bottom of the pool with his toes and puts them back on. He speaks first. "You don't have to tell me what happened. But whoever hurt you is an idiot."

I close my eyes and let the cool water pull the heat from my skin. The ache's still there—but it's not choking me anymore.

"Yeah," I say. "He is."

Patrick doesn't say anything right away. He floats beside me, his sunglasses dripping.

"For what it's worth," he says, voice lower now, "if you ever want to talk—or just swim and not talk—I'm around."

For the first time, he isn't posturing or acting arrogant. He's not trying to be clever. He seems to be offering something real.

"I'll keep that in mind," I say.

He nods, pushes off the wall, and floats on his back, arms out like a mannequin in Sunday clothes tossed into the deep end.

"Hey," I call out. "I thought you said you couldn't swim."

"Nah," he says. "I said I didn't like cold water. It's nice and warm in here today."

Patrick mumbles under his breath, "What kind of fuckin' moron thinks a kid with a pool doesn't know how to swim?"

29

No Place For Me

Naomi is out of town visiting her mom and sisters in Macon. Mateo is working at the diner each morning and pulling doubles at Burkhart's all weekend. I tried making plans with both, but no luck.

That's fine, probably for the best. I'm not going out. No Burkhart's, no Anvil, no Steamworks. No cruising or hookups either, no matter what opportunities present themselves. This weekend will be a quiet time devoted to and for myself. I'm staying in and finally taking control—proof that I still can.

I shave and get dressed. I tell myself I need to get out of the apartment and get some fresh air that doesn't involve being in the sun or cleaning someone else's stuff. I'll go somewhere familiar, somewhere I'll enjoy myself and won't have to explain anything to anyone, so I head to B-Side Records. Maybe I'll sort the new arrivals or alphabetize the jazz section again—something slow and simple. It's not exciting. Not glamorous. But it's mine.

The bell above the door gives its usual half-hearted jingle as I enter. The air smells like dust and sleeves of old plastic. It's cool and cozy, and jazz plays softly from the back speakers—Coltrane, probably. Something wistful and low because it knows exactly where my head is right now.

I nod to Eddie at the register. "Just here to hang. You good?"

"Yeah, man," he says. "No rush. Just got a weird rush earlier—Saturday tourists from Marietta, I think," he chuckles. "Place just cleared out again."

"They buy anything?"

"Ah, hell no," Eddie laughs again. "You know them cats don't own no turntable."

I smile and nod in agreement. Eddie has owned the place for decades, long before the big chains like Peaches Records or Camelot Music took over the malls. B-Side Records is an expansive space with large factory windows and high ceilings with exposed ironwork. It was once part of an auto assembly factory. Now, it's filled with vinyl and tapes and even features a few recording studio booths in the back for artists. Serious audiophiles come to see Eddie, as do recovering young men seeking great tunes to help them get their lives back on track.

Yeah. This is precisely what I need today. Not a distraction—balance.

I move toward the back wall in the corner, to the section where Eddie stashes the imports and rarities. I like it there. It's quiet and tucked away. Fingers trail across spines already memorized—not reading, just scanning—letting the movement keep my hands busy while I decide where to start. The jazz section calls next. There's no rush. The whole day lies ahead to relax and do as I please.

The bell jingles again.

A casual glance—probably just another regular to trade or tap into Eddie's knowledge and experience. Maybe it's someone I know. But then I see them, and freeze.

Kevin walks in, and he's not alone.

Josh enters just behind him, laughing about something and playfully elbowing Kevin. Kevin smiles—wide, easy, the kind of smile I haven't seen since that night in Bayview. They move together comfortably as if it's routine. Josh leans in to whisper something, and Kevin shakes his head, still grinning. There's no tension. No weight. Just two people who fit.

I don't move. I'm standing too exposed where I am, a Coltrane reissue in one hand, and my breath caught somewhere between my ribs. But they haven't seen me yet.

Kevin pulls an album from the bin and leans forward to say something. Josh smiles at whatever it is, his whole body in it. Their heads are closer than I've ever seen them. And then they kiss.

When I see it, my heart lurches with a spike of adrenaline. My first instinct is to walk up and say something. Anything. *You lied to me. You promised to meet me, but didn't show up. You kissed me and said you remembered.* Part of me wants to look Josh in the eye and ask him what he thought would happen after calling me at work like that.

My feet even take a step forward, but I stop. Confronting them wouldn't reclaim anything. I was never the one.

That's when the music changes. The low hum of whatever was playing fades into a soft, sorrowful trumpet line. I recognize it immediately. Chet Baker.

"I'm a fool to want you..."

My eyes shut. Of all the fucking songs.

"To want a love that can't be true..."

When I open them again, Kevin's gaze is drifting toward the back, scanning the bins—and then it happens. His eyes land on me.

We lock gazes and hold them for a second, maybe less. I expect Kevin's eyes to soften. Maybe a half-smile or at least a nod, a signal that something's still there. Anything.

Instead, he turns away. The motion is deliberate and clean, like a period at the end of a sentence.

He places a hand gently on Josh's back. It's not a casual touch. It's a gesture of care—fingers resting on Josh's lower back, below his shoulder blades, and above his waist. Kevin is rubbing small circles of comfort, caressing him, as he leans in to whisper something only Josh should hear. Then Kevin laughs, extends his arm around Josh's hips, and leads him farther down the aisle.

Like I was never here.

Standing there motionless, the air inside me stills. Kevin saw me. He knows I'm here.

"I'm a fool to hold you..."

The blood pounding in my ears drowns out everything else. The shop shrinks around me. Chet croons through the speakers, and everything he sings is true.

I place the Coltrane record back on the shelf, careful not to let it slip out of my shaking hands. This was my place. My escape. My little world of secondhand noise and alphabetized meaning. But now Kevin's here, too—smiling, relaxed, at home in it. And he brought Josh into it.

I walk out wordless. No bell. No goodbye to Eddie. Just the door swinging closed behind me, sealing the scene like the end of a film I never wanted to watch.

"Time and time again, I said I'd leave you..."

But I didn't. I came back. But now I know.

I'm not a secret anymore. I'm the ghost. And ghosts don't belong in the daylight.

30

Secret Journey

T he door clicks shut behind me. For a second, I stand there—keys in hand, feet on the threshold like I haven't decided whether I'm staying or leaving again. The fan is off, so the air inside is stale from the heat. It smells like toast and this morning's coffee grounds when my day started so perfectly. There's also a low, dying hum in the air, something familiar yet unexpected. The turntable's platter still spins, even though the tonearm rests in its cradle—motion without sound, like something waiting to be remembered.

Outside, the drone of traffic up Piedmont Avenue and down Juniper Street creeps through the old window sills, a rasping chorus of movement rising and falling with the static of the turntable. Two different textures of emptiness layered together to fit as one.

I take a step forward. Then another. My shoes stay by the door, forgotten in the motion of entering, but I don't remember taking them off.

The filtered light through the north-facing windows is the color of overripe peaches—thick and low, catching the dust motes in the air like little ghosts suspended in honey. Everything looks softer than it is—like it's been blurred or waterlogged. Like someone's wiped their hand across the glass of a framed memory.

The living room still holds this morning's half-drunk glass of water, sweating on the coffee table, leaving a pale ring on the wood. I press my thumb into the circle to smudge it. Just to move something. The condensation is cool against the skin of my thumb, and it surprises me.

I sit, then stand again. The old couch that Naomi helped me find at a second-hand store feels too low to the ground. Too soft. I step over a laundry basket left by the bathroom and make my way to the bed, but don't lie down. Instead, I sit on the edge, my elbows on my knees, my hands hanging loose between them. The quiet rings in my ears, high and hollow.

Kevin was laughing.

That's the part that loops in my head. Not the way he looked away from me. Not his hand on Josh's back. Just the sound of his laugh. It wasn't forced, or awkward, or guilty. It was genuine and whole, but just not for me.

I rest my head in my hands. The heels of my palms press into my eye sockets until color bleeds through—reds, oranges, that violet static behind the lids when there's too much feeling and nowhere to put it.

Deep down, I know they are not the villains in my story. Kevin didn't betray me back then. Josh didn't steal anything. There wasn't a theft. There wasn't even a fight. There's just a vision of a life that I don't belong to.

The turntable still spins in the other room, yet there's no music, just a faint hum that sounds like rain falling on a distant roof.

There are no tears. No tension building behind my eyes, no pressure in my throat. Nothing to release. I wish there were. That would mean something was still alive in me. Something worth fighting for.

Everything feels weightless. Loosened from gravity. It's like sitting at the bottom of a pool—airless—watching light bend in ribbons just out of reach.

There's a stack of vinyl on the floor, sleeves poking out, bent at the corners. One of them—I think—was playing that night. The night of the swim. It was an obscure song by the Police. I don't remember the name—

No.

I do remember.

"Secret Journey." From *Ghost in the Machine.*

It played as I stood moonlit in front of his bedroom window, towel damp around my waist, trying to decide if staying meant becoming something I couldn't undo.

In that moonlit darkness, the lyrics spoke of seeing the light in the darkness of what was happening—of making sense of it—and when the evening's secret journey was completed, I would find the love I missed.

I didn't see the light, however.

I didn't stay long enough to.

Not that night. Not in Bayview. Not in Kevin's life.

I shift onto the floor, my back pressed against the bedframe, my knees up. I run a finger along the edge of a scuffed floorboard until it catches on a splinter. I don't pull away. I press harder.

There's no pain. Not really. Just the weight of being here. Just presence.

31

LIGHT IN THE DARKNESS

The room hasn't changed, but something in me has. It's darker now. The last of the daylight is gone, and the only illumination comes from the sodium-orange glow leaking in through the blinds. It cuts across the floor in angled stripes, the way it always does around this time. Everything looks amber and bruised.

I haven't moved much. A few feet, maybe, after dozing off at some point, sitting there, back against the bedframe. My hip is sore, and my right arm tingles where it went numb under my weight. Shifting, I rub my wrist and flex my fingers, but don't stand. There's no reason to.

I finally rise and walk barefoot into the living room to open a window halfway. Warm air slips in, not any cooler than what was already inside, but it carries sound—muffled laughter from someone's TV, the faint clink of glass from a porch down the block, and footsteps above me. Signs that life is still happening around me.

I cross the room and crouch by the stack of vinyl that leans against the bookshelf—some I bought, but most were trades from the shop. A few have become permanent—too scratched to sell yet too familiar to part with.

Flipping past the Talking Heads, Eurythmics, and Sade, I finally find it.

Ghost in the Machine.

The sleeve is creased at the corner, soft from wear. I hold it in both hands, not even pulling the record out yet. The artwork is simple—a black background with glowing red digits, like a digital face watching in silence. I once thought it was cold. Now it feels like something looking back.

I don't recall where or when I picked it up, only that it was one of a few Police albums he played that night. I remember the song playing low behind everything else—behind our breathing, his slow touch and soft kisses on my body, and my silence as soon as it was over.

Walking the record over to the turntable and kneeling, I lift the tonearm, and the vinyl lands gently on the platter. It spins slowly at first, then steadily. My fingers know the groove. I skip ahead, two tracks in. And there it is, the promise buried in the lyric: light in the darkness.

The speakers crackle for half a breath—then the synths begin. Gentle, spiraling, haunted. The first few notes fill the room like fog. The melody is soft but insistent, a thread pulled through time.

I sit back on my heels.

The moment it hits me isn't dramatic. There's no sharp gasp or flash of recognition. It is just a quiet collapse. The kind where memory unfolds like mist curling in through the cracks—slow, shapeless, and suddenly everywhere.

I see the guest room. His sleeping bag is in the corner—the towel around my waist. Kevin is in the doorway. That song is playing.

~

(Four Years Earlier)

Water drips off our bodies in liquid trails as we emerge from the pool and grab towels to dry off under the moonlight. The sliding glass door clicks behind us as the TV flickers, casting weird shadows across his aunt's snoring body on the sofa. She doesn't stir.

Kevin leads me down the hallway, barefoot and quiet, like he's afraid the floor might give us away. I follow, still damp and wondering if I'll regret this before it's over. That was the moment either of us could have stopped. Neither of us did.

The door softly closes behind us, and Kevin turns the lock. His room is sparse: a sleeping bag atop an air mattress on the floor, a short bookshelf, a turntable with speakers and a few albums, and bare walls illuminated by the amber glow of a streetlamp leaking through the blinds.

"Well," I say, "it's not The Ritz, buddy."

I feel beads of water drip from my tousled hair onto my shoulders and down my back, and he watches me like I'm something he's memorizing. Unsure what to do with that look, I turn away toward the quiet space between words where everything feels fragile and unfamiliar. I slowly loosen the towel around my hips, letting it drop to the floor.

"It may not be much," Kevin says, gesturing toward the makeshift bed, "but it's comfortable."

I don't rush. I let my hands slide down my sides, peeling Kevin's black Speedo down my legs in one slow, fluid motion. I step out of them, unhurried, and step toward the bed like I've done this before. I haven't. Not like this. Not with someone who looks at me like that. I kneel forward and stretch out on my stomach, wrapping my arms around the pillow and tucking it under my head. I don't say a word. I don't have to.

At first, I hear nothing but my blood pumping through my eardrums. I listen and hear the soft thump of Kevin's towel and wet shorts land on the floor. I can sense his eyes on my body, but it doesn't make me self-conscious—it makes me feel desired in a terrifying yet simplistic way. I don't know what to expect; I only know it's happening, so I lie there and hope Kevin does.

He climbs over me, straddling me, his knees on either side of my thighs. Then I feel his lips—barely there—on my shoulders and spine. He plants kisses on me slowly, tracing the length of my back. He eventually reaches my tan line and the baby-white softness on my buttocks below my waist. He ventures downward, brushing his lips lightly against the soft flesh below my waist with gentle kisses and a reverence I didn't expect.

My body tenses as I feel his chest brush against my back, and then relaxes again as his hands find mine beneath the pillow. He squeezes them gently—just enough to say, 'I'm here.'

Kevin keeps planting soft kisses on me. My neck. My ears. My back. His breath is warm against my skin, and then I feel him— his body resting against mine, warmth pressed into the small of my back and in the furrow of my two muscular cheeks. I tense at first, but slowly relax. The sensation of his body against mine sends a rush through me: overwhelming, new, impossible to imagine or ignore.

Kevin slowly lowers his body onto mine and pauses, resting motionless atop my exposed willingness, in the quiet space between us. I feel engulfed by him, like a warm, weighted blanket of skin and muscle—solid, steady, and safe—protecting me from the world.

"Mmm," I whisper. "That feels good." And it does.

Kevin doesn't rush. He doesn't take. He lets it all stretch between us—desire, fear, excitement—like he's memorizing me in the dark.

I wonder where he's learned to do this. Has he read books on the art of foreplay and lovemaking? Has he practiced each move on the women he's been intimate with? What he's doing, what I'm feeling, is uncharted territory for me. Should I roll over? Should I assert myself? No, Kevin is my guide, so I lie still and wait, simultaneously aroused and frightened.

Kevin holds me close to him and rolls us both onto our side. He's still behind me, his hand across my chest, our fingers now intertwined. He explores my chest in gentle circular motions with his fingertips, taking my hand along with his. I begin to take over, guiding him slowly and quietly down my chest, showing him what I want and where I need him. Every inch is new territory—across each nipple and every ribcage bone. I guide his fingers lower to trace the cuts between each abdominal muscle. His chest presses against me, and I feel his breathing shallow as his heartbeat quickens against my back.

The experience is raw, but there's a tenderness to it, a rhythm not to rush. It no longer feels unfamiliar. It feels inevitable.

The buildup is unbearable now. It's too much. Too slow. Too good. I hear my own heart pounding like the sexual drumbeat of a man about to go mad. My rapid and deep breathing matches Kevin's, and it feels like we are sharing a set of lungs. His chest and my back contract and expand in unison, meshing as one, running the same race together.

I feel his hand graze me there, hard, already slick with anticipation. I press into him. I want him to know he's allowed. My hand releases his, trusting him to cradle it, to hold me just right.

And he does.

His grip is perfect. Firm but careful. It's like he's trying to figure me out, not just get me off. I moan, soft and low. I don't care how loud I am. He needs to know he's doing it right.

My panting quickens, and as it does, I feel his unconstrained hardness press against the back of my legs and buttocks. He's making slow, rotating, grinding motions against me, and I reciprocate with involuntary gyrations of my hips. Each time I do, I can feel the faint exhale of his breath against my ears and neck.

He moves with instinct, like he's done this a hundred times, but still wants to get it right. I don't guide him anymore—I don't need to. His touch is confident and careful, learning me as he goes. Each stroke sends a deeper ache through me, answered by the sounds rising in my throat. It's permission. It is want. It's everything I didn't know I could ask for.

Eventually, Kevin moves, allowing my body to roll onto its back and settle into the warm space he just vacated. The lamplight from outside illuminates me, and Kevin uses it like a guide to find the rest of me. He hovers above, his weight supported by his hands and knees, and begins to plant soft kisses on my chest, alternating between gentle kisses, light licking, and gentle sucking. I arch up when he teases my nipples, and I can't stop the small sounds that leave my mouth. I've had sex before. But this is different. I feel seen.

Kevin trails down my body with his lips and tongue, stopping every few inches to taste, to breathe, to look. He plants exploratory kisses on my thighs, my hips, the space just beside where I want him to go.

It feels like he's dragging it out—teasing, testing me. Worshipping, maybe. Or maybe that's just how I want it to feel.

His arousal brushes against my skin, the warmth of it tracing along my thighs. Each time his mouth gets closer, my back arches in anticipation, hips lifting in silent urgency—hoping, aching for more.

But he doesn't. Not yet. He pauses each time and deliberately bypasses it, painfully stretching the pleasure by kissing my inner thighs and hips. This torture is not to rush—it's for every breath, every inch, every ache of wanting, and the slow burn of desire. I glance down and see the gleaming drops—evidence of how much I like this—trail to my lower abdomen, shining in the low light, impossible to mistake.

Then Kevin's mouth finally claims me, and the sensation is tender, consuming, and deliberate. I forget how to breathe.

It's not just good—it's overwhelming. Kevin's lips are soft, and his mouth is warm. His tongue moves like he's memorizing every inch. I moan louder, and he doesn't stop. He doesn't flinch. He holds the base with his hand and keeps going like he's hungry and wants me to feel everything. Broken sounds rise from my throat, and with every moan, Kevin takes a little more, swallowing me a little deeper.

I can't hold still. My hips move, and Kevin lets me. My whole body is on fire, and he knows precisely how to stoke the flames.

His rhythm increases, and I feel myself grow harder—degrees of hardness I didn't think possible—by the intensity of desire, the thrill of surrender, and the unrelenting pleasure of being consumed by someone else's need—without question or restraint.

I'm getting close and put my hands on his shoulders and neck, unsure if I should push him away or draw him in closer. But he doesn't stop.

My moans grow louder as my body begins trembling with unspoken urgency. My hips move on their own, chasing the rising wave of sensation building in me. My breath shatters—scattered, frantic—as I edge toward something I can't undo. I can't stop myself, and Kevin doesn't stop, either—until the very last moment.

My back arches instinctively, and I let go, every muscle trembling as release overtakes me. The waves come in pulses, tightening and relaxing my entire body, thin ribbons of pleasure coming from deep within, landing across my chest, the pillow, and even my hair. It's raw and strangely beautiful, leaving me breathless and undone as I grab the sheets that cover the sleeping bag and grip them tightly in my fists.

"Fuck," I moan. "Fuck, fuck, fuck."

It takes a few moments before I slowly ease my grip, my fingers uncurling in the aftershocks of the release. My consciousness returns sluggishly, and I begin to become aware of Kevin's presence again. He's still here, kissing my thighs, rubbing my legs, and grinning at his accomplishment—the trust, the need, the response.

I stare at the ceiling. I can feel my body relaxing; my chest is rising and falling, and my breath is returning to normal. "Damn," I say.

"Don't move."

His legs look unsteady as he stands and walks to the bathroom, still hard—engorged with unmet needs of his own. I hear water running. Kevin returns with a warm washcloth and kneels beside me, quietly wiping away the aftermath with a tenderness that catches me off guard. I lie still and let him. He's taking care of me—again—like it means something.

When Kevin finishes, he quietly disappears into the bathroom again. I hear him toss the cloth into the corner. And that's when I panic. By the time he returns, still naked and erect, I'm already standing, gathering my clothes.

"I gotta go, man. It's late." I've already got my shorts back on.

"You can stay if you want," Kevin says. "You don't have to rush."

"Thanks, but I really gotta go," I reply, slipping my shirt over my head. I can't make eye contact with him and realize I haven't since dropping my wet towel to the floor and lying face down on his bed.

"Hey, are you okay?" he asks, taking a step toward me and touching my waist.

"Yeah, I'm fine," I say. "It's just late." I don't mean to step back, but it happens.

"Okay, that's cool," Kevin says as he leans in for a kiss.

I look down when he does and turn away. I've got to get out of there—I can't breathe. I unlock the door and look back at Kevin with a tight, almost apologetic smile. "Call you later, buddy."

When I open the door and step into the hallway, I see his aunt still sleeping on the sofa. I glance back at him one last time and whisper, "See ya."

I never did.

32

THE RECKONING

The sky outside my window is the color of ash, with gray light bleeding into the corners of the room, as if it doesn't want to be here either. It looks like the remnants of something burned overnight—maybe my past, the memories with Kevin smoldered down to smoke and regret. There's no flame left to fan. All that's left is the wait to see what might rise from it. It's too early for birdsong and too late to go back to sleep, even on a Sunday.

I lay awake, but haven't moved in hours. One arm shields my eyes; the other rests across my chest. The sheet clings to dried sweat. My heart's not racing, it's just steady, like it's waiting for my mind to catch up to what it already knows.

The room smells faintly of skin and air that's gone still. My clothes are somewhere on the floor. The record player is silent. The world is silent. Just the faint tick of my watch on the nightstand beside me and the thin light through the blinds drawing pale lines across my chest.

Kevin didn't ruin me. That's the sentence that finally lands.

I've been building that lie for years, blaming what we did that night for my breakup with Stacy. For coming out. I blamed him for the moment I ran, for the way our friendship ended, and for the life he lived after I was gone. I used it to justify the hookups and the ache of not having a close relationship. I kept telling myself it was his fault—for exposing those emotions—and then moving on to someone like Josh. He didn't come looking for me. He didn't wait for me.

However, the truth is, he did. He opened the door. He asked me to stay, and I walked out. Josh didn't steal him. Kevin didn't break me or change me. I left.

That night. That version of him. That version of myself. I walked out and left it all behind, convincing myself I could chase it down later if I chose—as if it would always be out there, frozen in time, waiting for me to be ready.

But it wasn't.

Kevin is happy. Josh is kind. They laugh together. That version of him—the one I once believed was meant for me—was never mine. I only watched it from the outside, convincing myself I had a claim. But that life belongs to who Kevin is now, and I'm not part of it. I'm not the reason he smiles like that.

The version of Kevin I've been chasing all this time—it wasn't real. It was a memory softened by longing. It was a night I tried to preserve so I wouldn't have to confront who I became after it.

I wasn't running from Kevin that night. I was running from myself. Who I really was.

Closing my eyes, the thought settles. It doesn't feel like forgiveness. Not yet. But it's something quieter. Like space. Like breath. It's like the first moment after crying when your body realizes there's nothing left to cry over.

I don't need closure from Kevin. I need to stop leaving myself behind every time things get real.

Sitting up slowly, my back aches, and my legs are stiff. The window catches more of the morning light now, still soft and filtered by the trees, but growing brighter. I watch it climb the wall as if it's trying to remind me that time keeps moving, whether I want it to or not.

The bed's a mess. The air is still heavy. Nothing's really changed—but something in me has.

I'm not sure what comes next. But maybe, for the first time, I don't need to chase it. Perhaps I can let it find me.

33

FLIP TURN

The light is different later in the afternoon. It's less gray, less haunted. It's still soft but warmer—the kind of sunlight that feels like a truce.

Getting out of bed, I open the windows. Air stirs through the apartment, slow and stale at first, then cooler. The sheet stays where it fell, tangled on the floor like a skin no longer needed. The smell of myself lingers: sweat, sleep, and old emotions. I strip the bed, throw the sheets into the wash, and then shower before dressing, without having any specific plans for where to go or what to do. Right now, it's just about movement.

I pull out the small knapsack Naomi gave me from a book fair she attended and throw in a swimsuit, an extra T-shirt, and a folded towel. A borrowed copy of *Giovanni's Room* from Naomi goes in, too. On my way out, I glance once at the kitchen counter and see Kevin's number still sitting there, folded. No need to touch it. Not right now.

The streets are quieter on Sunday afternoons. The air hangs in that in-between stage of hot but forgiving. By the time I reach Piedmont Park, my shirt clings to my back. The weight of the sweat is a grounding reminder that this is real, that I'm present, not running from anything or rehearsing some conversation that'll never happen.

The park is packed with people, although the pool house is less than a quarter full by this time of day. It turns out to be Jazz

Festival weekend—not something noticed until I arrived. Laughter echoes off the concrete as a group of kids cannonballs into the shallow end. An older man reads a magazine in the shade. No one looks at me like I don't belong, which I'm okay with. I'm not here to be seen by others.

Finding a chair by the edge, I peel off my shirt and sit down to catch my breath. *Just breathe.* The water sparkles. It's not seductive, nor symbolic. It's just water. The sound of performers drifts in from the grassy center of the park. First, Etta James, then Dave Grusin, followed by Hiroshima. It's a who's who list of contemporary jazz greats, and I recognize them all as I tilt my head back and listen, soaking in the afternoon sunshine. It's not the same heat I endure when cleaning pools—this is the kind of warmth that rejuvenates you as you relax.

When I slip into the pool, entry is slow. The water bites at first, and my skin tightens in surprise, but I don't rush it. I sink under and let the water close over me, holding me without erasing me. When I surface, I don't gasp.

I just breathe again.

There are three swim lanes roped off with floats, and one is open, so I take it. Laps come easier than expected. I don't race. Instead, I swim casually down the lane and back again. My arms remember the rhythm despite not having swum in years, except when I met Kevin at Emory last month. Has it been five weeks already? It seems like it has been longer—and like no time at all, like the version of me who swam that day is still treading water somewhere.

At the deep end, I pause before the flip turn. Treading water, eyes tilted toward the sky, like I'm asking permission to come back different. The sun breaks through the clouds like it's been waiting for me to notice it. I smile. It's a small one, but it's real, and no one needs to see it.

I switch to breaststroke until my muscles ache in a good way. Until the tension in my chest feels looser. Until I feel like I'm part of something again, not a person watching life from a distance.

Back on the concrete, wrapped in a towel, I sit in the last of the day's sunlight and let the breeze brush my skin to dry it. My thoughts drift to Naomi and Mateo. It's been a while since I've cooked something other than hot dogs or eggs. Maybe I'll go home and listen to albums. I'm not sure yet.

Somewhere behind me, a saxophone trails off into applause, and a breeze lifts the edge of my towel like a quiet reminder that I'm still here. Here, but no longer drowning in the question. Whatever's unresolved, it can come or go. I'll be here either way. I'm not chasing it. Not anymore.

34

The Confession

A single candle flickers on the table—something I don't usually bother with. The apartment smells of garlic and thyme. I'm not sure what possessed me to cook an authentic meal—maybe it was yesterday's decision at the pool, somewhere between sunlight and slow, steady flip turns. Swimming has always cleared the static in my head. Or maybe I just needed tonight to feel different. Not like me from the past few weeks.

Naomi knocks exactly twice as she lets herself in. "You trying to romance us or get rid of the roaches?" she says when she sees the candle.

"It's called ambiance."

"Mm-hmm," she says, kicking off her sandals and leaving them by the door. "Smells good. Are you trying to seduce Mateo?"

"He should be so lucky," I mutter, wiping my hands on a towel. "Been there, done that."

"Boy, please," she replies. "From what I hear, it wasn't that good. And yet, speak of the devil; here he is with Coke and regrets."

Mateo walks in carrying a six-pack of Coke and a bag of chips, which he clearly didn't think through. "Sorry, I panicked," he says. "This was all they had at the bodega."

"You walked past a damn Kroger," Naomi says flatly.

"I didn't say it was the nearest bodega."

We eat at the small round table under the kitchen light—pasta with sautéed mushrooms and way too much black pepper. Mateo frowns after the first bite, then goes back for seconds. Naomi doesn't say anything; she eats and then gets up to grab another bottle of cheap wine from my cabinet as if she lives here.

The jokes taper off after a while, replaced by a silence that feels more like awkward waiting than a pause in conversation.

"I need to tell you both something." I clear my throat.

Naomi sets her glass down gently. Mateo leans forward, arms crossed on the table like he's bracing himself.

I haven't rehearsed what I want to say, and I know it won't come out perfectly, so I start slow. The truth will be enough for now, though.

"Kevin's boyfriend, Josh, called me at work last week after the holiday. It was weird. He wasn't angry; he just asked me when Kevin and I reconnected and how long it had been going on, whatever 'it' was. He said he 'saw me.' It was kinda a polite warning, I guess."

They don't interrupt, which surprises me.

"Then Kevin calls the next day," I continue. "He freaked out when I told him Josh called me; he said he didn't know anything about it. I was mad as hell at him. I forced him to agree to meet me on Friday, to explain himself—why he led me on and then wanted nothing to do with me."

Naomi's eyes flick to Mateo, sharp with concern. He looks like he's holding in ten questions at once, but neither of them says a word—they just let me speak like they know this part needs air before anything else.

"Well," I say, "he never showed."

Naomi exhales hard as if she's trying not to say, 'I told you so,' but can't quite hide it. Mateo shakes his head slowly, eyes narrowed—not angry, exactly, just disappointed on my behalf.

I take a deep breath and continue. "Long story short, Kevin and Josh came into B-Side Saturday while I was there. Kevin saw me—I don't think Josh did."

Mateo sat up straight. "What the hell were they doing there?" He looked like he'd just witnessed a neighbor that he hated let their dog shit all over his prized zinnias.

"Same thing we do. Look at vinyl."

"Well, what happened?" Naomi anxiously asked.

"Nothing," I replied. "I left. Angry. Kevin looked right at me and then turned to put his arm around Josh, leading him away. He might as well have given me the finger."

"You just left?" Mateo asked.

Naomi put up a hand and told him to "shush."

"I kept telling myself it was a coincidence—that seeing them didn't mean anything. That I didn't feel anything. But I did. I came home and spiraled, as usual, and spent the rest of the weekend sleeping, cleaning, and thinking."

I pause and contemplate continuing. Where am I going with this? I gaze at Naomi, and her eyes are soft. Mateo's thumb is tapping against the side of his glass.

"I didn't tell you everything before. Back then, in Bayview—about the last time I was with Kevin. It wasn't just a friendly moment. It was *the* moment. We swam. We kissed. We—" I stop. *Just say it*, I tell myself. "We had sex, but it was more than just physical. Kevin was my first. It scared the hell out of me when it was over."

There it is. The sentence I never let myself say out loud. It hits the air like surfacing after a long dive—quiet but deep. I just let myself breathe.

Naomi lets out a deep breath herself. Mateo shifts slightly, his expression unreadable.

"I blamed him for everything that went wrong after. I built my entire identity around that night and never once took responsibility for what I did. For leaving. For hiding. For turning into someone who doesn't know how to stay."

For a second, neither of them moves. Naomi's hand squeezes her glass, her jaw tight but her eyes warm, like she knows this part cost me something. Mateo glances down, then back up, his expression softer than I've ever seen it. Not pity, but rather understanding.

I continue. "I don't know what I want from Kevin anymore," I say, "but I know what I don't want. I don't want to chase a version of him, or myself, that doesn't exist. I don't want to keep mistaking longing for direction. I just want to be honest. With him. With myself."

Naomi tilts her head, studying me. "You're different tonight," she says.

Mateo adds, "Sounds like you flipped a switch. Or flipped one off."

I look down at my plate. There's still food left, but I've lost interest in eating.

Naomi reaches across the table and lays her fingers lightly on mine. "You don't have to be perfect to be honest, baby. You only have to mean it."

"Wow," Mateo nods. "So what now?"

"I'm thinking of writing him a letter. No pressure. No agenda. Just tell him the truth about what happened. Finally."

They don't answer right away. I watch their faces as the thought settles.

"Do it," Mateo says. "Say what you need to say. Then walk away."

Naomi leans back. "Closure's a scam," she says. "But honesty? That shit will set you free."

I can't help but chuckle. It's a genuine one—small, tired, and grateful. "Are you two always this wise, or am I just finally listening?"

"We've been waiting for you to catch up," Mateo says.

Naomi raises her glass. "To turning points. Even the messy ones."

We all clink. There are no big speeches—no movie moment— just the candle burning low and the feeling that I'm not carrying this alone.

35

THE LETTER

The bell jingles as the door swings open—half of me hoping Eddie's here, half hoping he's not. It's a bright, cracked sound that always feels too cheerful for a place full of traded and discarded things. Inside, the air smells like dust, vinyl, and something warmer—burnt coffee maybe, or Eddie's clove cigarettes.

Eddie glances up from behind the counter, adjusting his glasses. "Look what the cat dragged back. Didn't think I'd see you until Saturday."

"I need a favor," I say, not wasting any time and glancing around to ensure no one is here. It's midday in the middle of the week, so it's just the two of us.

He raises an eyebrow. "You don't need a job, do you? Cause I've already filled my quota of moody part-timers this decade."

A quick shake of the head answers him. "Nothing like that. I only need an address if you have it."

He watches me for a moment, then leans back in his chair. "You asking as Daniel, my vinyl-loving customer, or Daniel, a heartbroken twenty-something who's about to do something stupid he'll regret?"

A chuckle slips out to keep things light. "Both, but it's not that bad."

He sighs and rolls his chair over to the inventory cabinet. "Name?"

"Kevin Summers."

There's a pause—just long enough to make me wonder if this is a terrible idea.

"Special orders?"

"Yeah." It's the only reason he might have the address.

Eddie fingers his way past the R's and into the S's. "Yep. Here we go. A month ago. George Benson's *Breezin'*. Damn classic— can't keep used ones in stock. I remember him now. Tall, quiet. Kinda polite."

"That's him."

"Yeah," Eddie adds. "Had a conversation about 'This Masquerade.' The guy knew the track number, length, everything. Said it had the best piano interlude ever written and performed."

The track was familiar, and I knew its lyrics—Kevin played it for me back when we worked together. On slow nights before closing, we'd slip up to the stereo showroom, and he'd play his favorites for me.

'*Listen to how it pulls back instead of going flashy. It breathes,*' Kevin told me, explaining how the pianist used space and restraint. He talked about the modulations and key changes, explaining how the key subtly shifts to create emotional tension. '*That shift into the chorus? That's not just a mood change—it's harmonic. It's a modulation that lets the melody ache a little deeper.*'

'*Real jazz stuff mirroring emotional distance,*' he'd say. '*Built to linger.*'

I didn't understand it fully at the time. I just knew that when we sat there in the high-end audio room, with the lights dimmed low and George Benson's voice drifting out of the speakers, it felt like something real was being said—and not just by the music.

Maybe the special order was for Kevin to play it for Josh, to say the same things with the same passion. Perhaps it was for himself to remember me. It doesn't matter now—not anymore.

Eddie scribbles an address on a small pad. "You didn't get this from me."

I nod and take the slip. "Thanks."

"Don't do anything stupid."

~

The kitchen table sits quiet, a pen and pad resting in front of me—unfinished, unsigned. The light outside fades, but I sit still, as if I move too soon, the words will scatter. I read the letter once, then again. The handwriting is neat and deliberate.

Kevin,

I'm not sure what I expect this to do. I just know I need to say it. That night changed me. Not in the way I always feared it would, but in a way I never understood until now. You were the first person who really saw me, not who I was trying to be, but who I was underneath. That terrified me, and I ran.

For a long time, I blamed you for everything that followed—for what I felt, what I didn't, and what came after with Stacy. But none of that was your fault. You didn't ruin me. You opened a door. I was the one who closed it. I'm sorry I ran.

I'm not asking anything of you. I just want to say thank you for letting me be myself for the first time. For one night. I think I've been trying to get back to that person ever since.

You've built something good with Josh. Something real. I hope I will someday, too.

—Daniel

The letter folds slowly in my fingers, and I slip it into an envelope that remains unsealed—for now, for reasons not quite clear. Tomorrow, I'll deliver it. Not because I want something. Because it's time.

~

It's not a grand gesture. It's more like a quiet step—a follow-through. No expectations. Just the quiet urge to stop carrying it.

The neighborhood smells like jasmine and grill smoke, the kind of summer evening where the air carries a stillness that makes you second-guess everything. I park a block away and stroll to the house number. I don't want to startle anyone, or to seem like I'm here for a fight—just the opposite.

The envelope's in my hand, bent slightly from how tightly I've been gripping it. I take a breath, then another. I almost turn around, but I'm at the door.

The house is quiet. There's a light on in the front room. I knock, and after a moment, there are footsteps. Then the door opens—but it's not Kevin.

Josh blinks at me. His blond hair is damp, and his feet are bare. He's wearing a T-shirt and shorts, comfortable and composed, more so than I would be in the same circumstance, but there's hesitation in his eyes. He looks like he's bracing for something he already half knows.

"Daniel?"

I nod. "Hi. Sorry. I just wanted—Kevin's not home, is he?"

He shakes his head slowly. "He's got class tonight. He'll be home in a couple of hours. Why are you here?"

"Right," I say, my voice catching on the word. I begin to raise my hand, but stop. "Would you—do mind if I come in? Just for a minute. I want to give him something, but I can leave it with you."

Josh studies me. I can tell he's debating whether to slam the door in my face out of surprise and anger or let me in out of curiosity. Then he steps aside. "Sure."

The house feels newly lived in, as if the furniture is there, but nothing has settled in. There's a record shelf against one wall—nothing playing. A faint citrus scent lingers in the air. Josh leads into the living room, and I trail after. He gestures toward the couch but doesn't sit.

I remain standing also.

"I'm not here to start anything," I say quickly. "I just—I wrote Kevin something. A letter."

Josh nods slowly. "About what?"

"About everything." I raise the envelope, a silent offering. "I just wanted him to have it. That's all."

He takes it but doesn't look at it. For a moment, I wonder if he'll rip it up right in front of me. At the very least, I know he'll read it before giving it to Kevin. That's what I would do. "You're not trying to—"

"No." I cut in gently but firmly. "I'm not trying to restart anything. Or ruin anything. I know what you and Kevin have. I'm not here to get between that."

Josh watches me for a long moment, his expression unreadable. Then, softly: "I can tell you were important to him."

A silent nod follows. "Kevin was important to me, too. But that doesn't mean I get to rewrite what happened. I don't want to. I just needed him to know the truth of why I did what I did."

He turns the envelope in his hand, eyes flicking between me and Kevin's name written on the envelope. "I haven't seen him like that in a long time—after he saw you Saturday. It rattled him."

My surprise stays hidden. I wonder if Josh saw me at B-Side, too. Questions rise inside me—what Kevin whispered, why they laughed, if Kevin played "This Masquerade" for him too—but none of them leave my mouth.

"I know," I say. "It rattled me, too."

Josh exhales, then carefully places the envelope on the console table by the wall. "I'll give it to him."

"Thank you."

As I turn, Josh's voice stops me cold.

"Was it worth it? Writing that?"

A beat passes. "Not sure yet. But it felt honest—more honest than I've been in a long time."

He nods once and sees me out. And just like that, I'm on the outside again, *'lost inside this lonely game we play.'*

36

THE HUSH OF DARKNESS

(Josh)

Kevin's beside me in bed, but it doesn't feel like he's with me. His back is turned to me, shoulder bare above the sheet, rising and falling with each slow breath. He came home late from class, tired and quiet, and mentioned that a group presentation had run longer than expected. I didn't press. I never do.

The letter is still in the drawer of the entry table. I haven't given it to Kevin yet.

Not yet.

I keep replaying what Daniel said to me. Not the words exactly—though some stuck—but the tone. The steadiness of it. The truthfulness of it.

He wasn't trying to convince me of anything—not even trying to win Kevin back. He didn't say anything about closure either. He just seemed to need to tell his truth out loud.

Which makes it harder to dismiss—harder to ignore.

Kevin shifts slightly, curling in on himself the way he does when he's holding something in. I think of all the times I've felt that distance before and told myself it was just stress. School. Work. The move.

But maybe it was always this.

Daniel said he needed Kevin to know the truth about why he left. I assume he meant what happened in Bayview—the night they had sex. I know Daniel is the boy Kevin told me about when we first met—when we talked in that diner for hours on end, getting to know one another.

I haven't read the letter, but I also don't know how or when I'll give it to Kevin. I assume it contains all the things Kevin never told me—and maybe all the things he never planned to.

The lamp gets switched off, casting the room into a hush of darkness.

I want to believe Kevin's silence is merely caution. I want to think this doesn't mean anything. But wanting and knowing are not the same thing. Still, I lie awake and wonder what else I haven't asked—and what he's still not saying.

37

THIS MASQUERADE

While restocking supplies behind the front counter, I spot him through the window. Kevin is standing just outside the store, hands in his pockets, looking nervous, like he's not sure if he's here for me or just hoping I'll see him first.

Instinct pulls me back. My heart tightens—not racing, just bracing for what is about to happen.

Kevin steps inside, letting the door close behind him. It's a warm morning, but he looks like he's been holding his breath since yesterday. He looks different—not physically different, just unsure, like someone trying to change the ending without rewriting the beginning.

He must have read it. Or maybe Josh said something. I don't ask.

"Hey," he says.

"Hey." I don't offer more.

He walks up to the counter, avoiding my eyes at first, then meeting them like he realizes he has to.

"I'm sorry I didn't show up or call. I—I should have."

A nod. "It doesn't matter."

"No, no. It does matter." He studies me. "I wanted to. I still do. I miss talking to you."

It lingers between us. That old magnetic pull. Familiar. Dangerous.

"I've been thinking," Kevin says, his voice lower. "Maybe we could keep hanging out. Meet for swims. Not like—not the way it started. But as friends. Just us. Like before."

"Before what?" I ask.

He hesitates. "Before it got complicated."

It's still complicated, but I don't say that. I wait.

"Josh doesn't have to know," he adds too quickly.

That's when I know. It hits me—not how much I wanted Kevin, but how long I mistook wanting him for something deeper. I thought he had changed, too.

My stomach knots. Not with desire but with grief. Did Josh give him the letter? Did he read it? I don't ask. Instead, I take a slow breath and step out from behind the counter.

"Kevin," I offer gently. "You should go home."

He blinks. "What?"

"You need to talk to Josh. Not me."

"But I came to see you."

"I know. But you're not here for me. You're running from something, and I won't be the place you hide."

He exhales sharply as if he might argue, but doesn't.

"What we had that night was real," I say. "And it mattered, but it's not who we are anymore. I'm done chasing ghosts. And I won't let you chase me to avoid your truth."

He stands there for a moment. Quiet. Looking down at his shoes, then at me. Kevin turns to go, pausing at the door. The light from outside makes his shoulders look heavier than I remember.

"Daniel?"

"Yeah?"

"I wasn't lying that night. I was ready. I really was."

I nod. "But I wasn't. And now it's your turn to be honest."

He opens the door. Sunlight spills in, and then he's gone.

Back behind the counter, I return to restocking. For the first time in a long while, it feels like I walked away from something I once wanted—and did the right thing.

38

THE STILLNESS AFTER

The sun is high and stubborn by the time I unlock the Phillips' side gate. Everything clings to the heat—the gate lock, the stone patio, even the lounge chairs I realign out of habit. July in the South is thick with everything—humidity, bugs, memories. The water's surface is motionless, like it's been waiting for me all day, a flat mirror of sky and clouds and the thoughts of my run-in with Kevin this morning.

The hose uncoils easily in my grip, and routine takes over—skimming the surface, checking filters, sweeping tile lines. It's automatic. My hands know what to do, which makes it harder for my mind to stay focused and keep from drifting.

The ache is quieter now. Not the sharp kind that screams, but worn, smoothed at the edges like a river stone. I used to think someone else had to pull it out—to name the pain, to fix it. But that's not how healing works.

Kevin showed up this morning, offering me a place to hide inside his shadow. He didn't mention the letter. And Josh—yesterday—offering something like peace without saying it. No blame. No anger. Just grace.

I thought I wanted him. Or clarity. Or closure. But standing there, watching him tuck his hands into his back pockets the way he always did when he didn't know what to do with his heart, all I could think was: we missed our moment. But maybe that's all it ever was—a moment. And perhaps that's enough.

A thin line of dirt clinging to the grout won't give. The brush jerks in my hand, but I keep going. Everything has to be clean.

The truth is, I spent almost four years fixated on a memory, feeling guilty for avoiding him and believing that if I could explain myself, everything would realign. But that night, after the swim, I didn't run out because I didn't enjoy what we did, or didn't want to be with him. I left because I did, and I didn't know what to do with that. That wasn't his fault. And that one act doesn't make me broken.

The brush clatters down. Kneeling, I catch my reflection—sweaty, tired, older than twenty-four should look. But there's something steadier there now.

Kevin's forgiveness was never the point. The real work was mine to do. I needed to forgive myself, and maybe for the first time, I do.

The wind kicks up, scattering a few dried petals from tiny white crape myrtle and large red hibiscus flowers across the water. Petals drift—tiny lifeboats adrift on a still surface. I'm not where I want to be, but I'm still here, and that means something.

The back door opens.

Patrick steps out barefoot, shirtless in cutoffs, squinting against the sun. His hair's a mess, like he just woke up from one of those slow, tangled naps. There's a hesitation in his step when he sees me, like he didn't expect to interrupt anything.

"Hey," he says, scratching his neck, "you're late today."

"I had some unexpected delays this morning," I say.

"What are you doing next weekend?"

A blink. "Next weekend?"

"Yeah." He shrugs, casual but not careless. "You always look busy, so I figured I'd ask early."

Straightening up. "You asking for a reason?"

He smiles—tilted, boyish, almost shy. "They're showing *Rebel Without a Cause* at Chastain Amphitheater. I figured you should see it. I don't know—if you're not working or whatever it is you do at night. Maybe we could go together."

Something about the way he says it—unpracticed and hopeful—makes me want to smile, not for what it might mean, but for the fact that someone asked.

"Why?" I ask, curious about his choice of the word 'should.'

Patrick throws his arms up into the air. "Pool guy, are you serious? It's a classic. James Dean. A kid wrestling with identity, masculinity, and being misunderstood. Desperate for connection, but pushing people away out of fear and confusion."

"Did you just take a film course in school?" I ask, teasingly. I can't help but consider the irony—Kevin taking me to a gay film festival, and now this kid asking me to go with him to a queer-coded classic.

"Yeah, I did. What are you, psychic?"

Something in me softens, reminding myself to stay present in the now, not in the anxiety of the future or the pain of the past. "I don't know," I say honestly, "sometimes I think I must be."

Patrick grins. "Whatever. Let me know on Tuesday. The show is on Thursday night." He then heads back inside as if he didn't just crack something open.

The sun is beginning to dip behind the neighbor's tall oak when I finish packing up. Cicadas scream like they always do when summer's peaking. I lock the gate, toss my gear in the truck, and drive home with the windows down and the air conditioning blasting.

Back in my apartment, I pull open the windows, strip out of my work clothes, and let the evening settle over me. I start cleaning—nothing intense, just the kitchen counters, some laundry, sweeping the floor. I put on an album—Fleetwood Mac's *Mirage*—and let Stevie Nicks tell the truth in the background while I fold towels.

The music drifts through the apartment like a spell. "Gypsy" starts up, and I catch myself swaying, just a little, as I wipe down the counter. There's an old comfort in her voice—like she knows what it's like to want something beautiful and not know how to keep it.

I light a candle, toss my sheets in the wash, and scrub out the inside of the fridge door. Not because it needs it, but because I want to. Because it's mine.

No one's waiting. No one's coming. And still, I feel whole. No ghosts. No pretending. For the first time in a long time, Friday night feels like mine.

39

SUSPENDED IN THE QUIET

I t's been four weeks since I handed Josh the truth and let Kevin go, and not a word from either of them. Mateo and I have visited B-Side several times, sometimes to browse, sometimes to loiter near the jazz section, but Kevin's never there. Some Saturdays, I wander in alone, pretending to shop, scanning the floor. Nothing. No sign of Kevin, no trace of Josh. They must've vanished into their old life while a new one slowly takes shape around me.

Still, I haven't regressed. No bars. No Steamworks. No reckless hookups to silence the noise. Just quiet days and quieter nights, slowly learning how to sit with the silence that's mine.

In that time, Patrick and I have found a quiet rhythm—unlikely friends orbiting the same city in different ways. I went with him to see *Rebel Without a Cause*, and after that, seeing him once a week became a kind of habit. A walk through Piedmont Park, a trip to B-Side to talk music, and a late-afternoon swim at the Y. Nothing big, nothing defined. But consistent enough to feel like he was more than just a client's son and a teenage smart-ass—like someone I didn't have to chase to feel seen.

The air outside is thick with heat, even as the sun begins to set. I sit with Patrick at a hole-in-the-wall Thai place off Cheshire Bridge Road, the one with sticky tables and spice-thick air that clings to your skin. The scent of basil, fish sauce, and grilled meat curls through the slatted windows, mixing with the faint tang of bleach from a half-mopped floor. The booth seats are cracked vinyl, the kind that peels against your thighs if you shift too much. A portable radio hums from somewhere near the kitchen, half-drowned by the hiss of a wok and the clatter of plates.

Patrick's twirling his noodles with plastic chopsticks slick from use, pretending not to watch me talk. The chopsticks click softly against the sides of his bowl as steam rises, fogging the glasses he wears when he doesn't have his contacts in. I don't say much at first. Just enough to keep things moving. But then I catch his eye and see he's listening—truly listening. So I tell him.

I talk about jogging in the morning before the humidity gets cruel, about swimming laps at the YMCA every chance I get, and about skipping bars and cutting back on drinking. I stay in more nights than not, and I feel clearer for it. The quiet times come more easily now. The clarity isn't constant, but it feels more honest.

Patrick raises his eyebrows. "So you're a complete bore now?"

I laugh. "Something like that."

He pokes at his food. "Don't you miss it? The scene? The action?"

"Sometimes. Then I remember what it feels like waking up with a hangover—sometimes alone, sometimes with a stranger and a gut full of regret."

He nods, biting back a smirk. "I wouldn't know."

"Believe me, it's better you don't."

"Sure," Patrick says, "easy for people who have done the bars and had the sex to say."

There's a part of me that wants to tell him he's not missing much, but I don't. He'll find his own way there. Everyone does eventually. And maybe he won't regret it as I do. Perhaps he'll make better choices, or maybe he'll recover faster.

Still, part of me wants to warn him, not from fear but from memory. From that hollow feeling that used to hit somewhere between the last call and the first break of dawn—when the noise fades, and all you're left with is sweat, smoke, and the ache of something that didn't happen, or something that did. But I know better than to hand someone a story that's not theirs.

After dinner, he assumes we're going out. He mentions a bar a few blocks down the road that he has heard of but has never been to. A place called Cityside, he says. I know the place all too well with its twink strippers and older daddies, its crowded dance floor, and naive out-of-towners from the rural parts of Alabama and Tennessee in town for the weekend looking for some gay action in the big city.

He looks so young, talking about it as if he's asking for permission.

A slow shake of my head. "I have a better idea."

We drive southeast, across town. The streets soften—more trees and fewer cars—until Midtown gives way to quieter neighborhoods. Patrick keeps glancing over like I'm leading him somewhere secret and illicit. Maybe, but not dangerous. We pull into the gravel driveway of the still vacant Scott Blvd. home and kill the engine. There are no lights, and the sign is still in the yard.

"Are we breaking into a house?" he asks.

"They know I'm here. I have a key."

"Why's it vacant?"

"The owners moved," I explain, "but I'm not so sure they're anxious to sell it."

We walk around back, and I unlock the gate. The pool is there, of course, and I flip on the submerged lights. The landscape lights come on, too, uplighting the trees and highlighting the yard's features. It's pretty, not as extensive or upscale as Patrick's backyard, but more intimate—more like a warm and cozy Italian country house. At the edge, I lower myself and dip my feet in. Patrick kicks off his sneakers, rolls his socks inside them, and then follows. The water laps against our ankles, warm and still.

"You swam here before?" he asks.

"Yeah, a few times. I clean it for them. Now they have me watch the house, too, for leaks and stuff like that."

Patrick leans back on his hands, looking at the night sky, and the silence between us stretches for a few minutes before he speaks.

"Sometimes I feel like everyone else got a head start. Like they got the manual, and I'm—I don't know—winging it."

A quiet nod as moonlight scatters across the surface. "Most people *are* winging it," I reply. "You get better at hiding the panic over time."

He exhales with half a laugh. "Do you ever stop feeling behind?"

"Not always, but sometimes. You catch up to yourself. These days, that's good enough."

He looks over at me, not smiling exactly, but with a soft grin, like he's still figuring out if I'm messing with him or telling the truth.

Standing, I tug my shirt over my head and fold it neatly, setting it beside the pool's edge. I step out of my jeans, leaving just my briefs. The air is cooling, and the water looks calm, inviting in a way that has nothing to do with desire and everything to do with presence—a kind of mirror waiting to be disturbed.

I glance at Patrick. He's watching—not staring, not smirking— just taking it in like he's not sure what this is but trusts it enough not to ask.

I slip into the pool slowly, without ceremony, the water rising across my body until it meets my chest. It's cool at first, then warms as I settle in. It's quiet and familiar. The kind of stillness you only get in a pool that hasn't seen kids or chaos for years. I push off from the edge and float on my back, held by the surface.

For a minute, it's just me—drifting.

When I open my eyes, Patrick is still sitting at the edge, elbows on his knees, watching with a soft kind of focus. Not awe—just a quiet sort of attention, like he's seeing something new.

A moment later, I hear a soft rustle, then the light scrape of his bare feet against the concrete.

Still, I wait—letting him decide.

Patrick pulls his shirt over his head, revealing his wiry chest still marked with the last traces of boyhood. His jeans come off next, then he steps in slowly, sucking in air at the temperature change before letting himself sink into the water and drift toward me, careful not to get too close at first.

We float quietly alongside each other, a few feet apart, eyes on the sky and occasionally each other. There's no music, no voices from nearby yards, just the low hum of cicadas and the hush of water displaced by our bodies and brushing against our skin.

His breath is audible, the space between us thinning. It's not sexual, not even flirtatious. Just two people suspended in the quiet—nothing to prove, nothing to chase.

We drift a little. Patrick kicks into the deep end and dunks under the surface, then surfaces and shakes his head like a dog. His hair slicks back, and his face and shoulders gleam under the lights.

"You ever feel like you're faking it?" he asks, voice low. "Not the being gay part—that part's real. But the whole swagger thing. The don't-give-a-shit thing."

I glance toward him. "Sometimes."

He nods slowly. "Yeah. That's most of my day—at school, at home. Walking into rooms like I'm untouchable. As if I'm fearless and know exactly what I want. Like I'm choosing everything— when really, I'm just trying to stay one step ahead of feeling anything at all."

Patrick laughs under his breath, but there's no humor in it. I know exactly how he feels. I tread closer, not touching him, but closer.

"I flirt with guys like it's a game," he says. "Tease, push—just far enough to feel something, but not enough to let it get real." And the whole time, I'm acting like I'm in control." He glances at me. "You ever done that?"

I hesitate, then nod.

Patrick exhales. "It's exhausting. But it's safer than saying what I really want. Because if I do, and I don't get it—it's not just rejection—it's confirmation. That I'm too much. Or not enough."

He sinks lower in the water, his chin barely above the surface. The pool is quiet. Just the faint sound of water lapping the edge.

"I think I act cocky so people don't ask," he continues. "So they don't see I'm still figuring it out. Like—am I looking for a boyfriend, or love, or just someone to make me feel less invisible? I don't even know the difference sometimes."

"I think you know the difference," I say.

Patrick looks at me for a long time. Not flirty. Not teasing. Just quiet. Searching.

"Yeah," he says. "Maybe I do. I just don't trust it yet."

He floats closer and nudges my shoulder with his. I don't pull away. We drift like that until the water feels cooler on our skin.

The moonlight ripples across his face, soft and uneven, like nothing here is trying to be perfect.

We don't kiss. Not here. Not yet.

40

THE PROMISE OF PRESENCE

We dry off in silence, dressing in the dark with slow, unhurried movements. On the drive back to my apartment, we roll down the windows. The air feels cooler now, less oppressive—like something's shifted between us, or maybe just inside me.

Patrick is half-asleep in the passenger seat, hair still damp, eyes blinking slowly as if drifting between one world and the next. When we reach my building, he follows me upstairs without a word.

He showers first while I dig out a pair of boxers for him. I throw his damp clothes in the dryer and fold them neatly afterward—something I do more out of desire than expectation, the carefulness of someone who rarely has overnight guests.

When he comes out, he curls up on my couch. I hand him a blanket, though he doesn't pull it over himself just yet. He shifts onto his side, one arm tucked beneath the cushion, the other resting across his chest like he's keeping something in.

"You ever feel like this is it?" he asks. "Like this version of you is all there's ever gonna be?"

"Sometimes. But it wasn't always like this—not this good, I mean."

"No?"

"No," I reply. "There were nights I barely remember. Not because they were wild or anything—just empty. One quiet hour bleeding into the next. I slept in my car for two nights, once. Too ashamed to go back to my wife. Too ashamed to explain anything to anyone else."

Patrick turns toward me as I slide deeper into the chair next to him.

"You were married? Jesus. What were you, straight?" He pauses. "What happened?"

"Her name was Stacy. It was brief and foolish—barely out of high school. Eventually, I packed a bag, gave her the keys, and left. She cried, but I didn't. I think I was too numb—too cracked open to feel anything but the need to get out."

"Cracked open by what?" Patrick asks, his tone softer now.

I sigh deeply and hesitate. Do I want to discuss this now? With Patrick? I shift forward in the chair, resting my elbows on my knees and cupping my hands.

"Cracked open by a guy. By having sex with a guy. But mostly by the intimacy."

"What happened?"

"A friendship. A chance meeting a couple of years later. One night in the pool. Curiosity, sex, confusion, shame. Afterward, I broke up with Stacy. I couldn't go back to what I had been, but didn't know what I was, either."

"What did you tell her?"

"The truth. In fragments. Probably more than I owed her, but not enough to set either of us free. She filed for divorce six weeks later."

"Damn," he said, quietly holding what I said before responding. "Is that when you came out?"

I chuckle nervously. "No. Not really. But I wasn't in, either. I was somewhere in between. In a place I didn't have a name for yet."

"Sounds familiar," Patrick murmurs. "So what did you do? What changed?"

I lean back into the chair. "Not sure. I slept on a buddy's couch for a while. I got a job cleaning pools, so I didn't have to look at my dad's disappointment at the restaurant. I told myself it was temporary, that I just needed some space. But really, I was hiding from what I'd done, from what I wanted, from the parts of me I wasn't ready to claim. I kept to myself. Worked a lot. Smoked too much."

"That was in Florida, right?" he asks.

"Yeah," I say. Maybe it was the swim, or simply being here, in the stillness and comfort of my surroundings. I'm comfortable telling Patrick things I hadn't even shared with Naomi or Mateo.

"It wasn't until a year ago that I got this offer to relocate with Sunbelt as they expanded into Georgia. Atlanta felt like a way out—bigger, faster, easier to disappear into. I took it. Rented this place, started over with new friends, a new routine. Eventually... new nights, new escapades."

"So that's when you came out?" Patrick asks, like he's trying to pinpoint the moment everything shifts.

"Officially, yes," I say. I could tell him about blowjobs by overfriendly sales clerks in department store dressing rooms, or glancing eyes and validations over urinals at rest stops, or the other games straight guys play when they're figuring out they're not so straight after all. I don't say any of those things, however.

"Yeah," I repeat, "when I moved here. Not in one moment. It happened slowly. Quietly. The first time I went all the way, I drank enough to forget most of it. But there were good moments, too. Small ones—a good date, a stranger who didn't expect me to explain myself. It took time, but the feeling of wrongness and the guilt started to fade."

"I'm still in that part, I think," Patrick said softly.

I give him a smile born of both compassion and gratitude. I tell him that's how I met Mateo, and how realistic and kind he was. How he helped me stop apologizing so much, even if I didn't know what I was sorry for. I explain how, little by little, the version of me that lived in Bayview started to feel like someone else's memory. Like someone I knew once. Someone I left behind the night I ran."

"It must've taken a lot," Patrick says.

"You don't know it yet," I say, "but you're standing at the edge of the same kind of loneliness I wasn't sure I'd survive at your age." The kind that doesn't look like sadness, but rather motion without connection. Charm without grounding. Touch without tenderness."

"You think that's where I am?"

"Maybe," I reply. "I recognize the look of searching for something that feels like permission. To want more. To be seen and not punished for it."

Patrick's eyes look heavy. "I don't wanna be punished for it."

"You won't be. Not here."

I watch as he exhales—his breathing calm, surrendering to rest in my apartment, trusting me with the part of him that doesn't know how to ask for safety while craving freedom.

When I stand, I draw the blanket halfway up his body, his legs curled inward, his breathing slowed into a deep sleep. The lamplight brushes the sharp edges of his face, softening him into something quiet and vulnerable. He looks younger like this. Unarmored.

I don't go to bed right away. I stand barefoot in the kitchen, setting up coffee with two mugs for the morning. The scent is grounding, warm, and welcoming. It fills the space with a sense of routine—something solid to hold on to.

Glancing back at him from the kitchen, I see the curve of his jaw, the looseness in his limbs, the stillness that asks nothing of me. For the first time in a long while, I'm not tracing Kevin's shadow onto someone else, but seeing Patrick. Only Patrick.

I smile quietly. No need to fix anything. No story to force. No craving to belong. There's no script I'm clinging to, no chase I'm on, no past I'm trying to rewrite. Just this breath. This room. This moment.

41

Enough For Now

(Same Saturday, Not Far Away)

(Josh)

The letter sat in my sock drawer for almost a month, sealed and unassuming. It lived beneath a stack of unmatched pairs I never wear—close enough to touch, far enough to avoid. The name on the envelope—Kevin's name, written in Daniel's hand—became something I couldn't stop reading.

I wanted to open and read it a hundred times. A thousand times. But I waited, watched, and gave Kevin space to lie, to flinch, to fumble. I kept hoping he'd tell me himself, that he'd say something, anything. But silence has a way of hardening into something heavier.

Then, three days ago, while he was sorting through the mail at the kitchen table, I handed it to him without a word—just slid it across the tabletop like a receipt. He looked at his name on the front and went pale. He must have known immediately. Kevin didn't ask me how I obtained it or how long I've had it. I didn't need to explain; it was clear. We both knew it wasn't mine to open.

He said he would read it alone, so I nodded and walked away. That was three days ago. The letter now sits on Kevin's desk in the guestroom, unopened. Or so I assume.

Tonight, Kevin doesn't eat much. We picked up takeout from that Korean place on Tenth Street, and he barely touches the bulgogi. The plates get cleared in silence. I wash the dishes while he sits out back, staring into the butterfly bushes that border one corner of the deck. His fingers are tapping out some rhythm on the arm of the chair that only he can hear.

The house is still, just the hum of the refrigerator and the occasional groan of a settling floorboard. It's been like this for a while, weeks in fact—quieter between us than usual. Not hostile, not even cold. Just quiet. The pretending wears thin. The silence is harder for me to ignore.

When I finish the dishes, I dry my hands on a towel and walk outside. Kevin looks up but doesn't say anything as I sit beside him.

"Are you going to open it?"

He blinks like he wasn't expecting me to say it out loud. Then he glances back across the green grass.

"I've read it," he says. "Three times."

Just a nod. The ache in my chest tightens the longer I stay silent, like a pulled muscle that keeps spasming.

"It wasn't what I expected," he adds. "It wasn't dramatic or angry."

"No?" I ask.

Kevin looks at me. His face is tired, pulled down from something heavy. Guilt, maybe. Or grief. It's sometimes hard to tell the difference.

"It was honest," he says quietly. "Daniel didn't ask for anything. He apologized—just said what he needed to say—what he should have said four years ago. I think he's moved on, and somehow, that made it harder to read."

"Because it means you don't get to pretend there's something still unresolved?"

"Yeah, I guess," he admits.

A long stretch of silence falls over us again. I let it stretch this time. It's uncomfortable, but necessary.

Then I ask. "Is there anything you need to say?"

Kevin swallows and looks down at his hands. "I guess I was trying to reconnect with a memory I didn't understand. Part of me wanted closure, but another part of me just wanted—." There was a long pause. "I don't know what. Honestly, maybe it was just ego. I don't know, I'm sorry."

"And now?" I ask.

Kevin leans forward, elbows on his knees, rubbing his palms together like he's trying to warm them.

"Now I'm here. If you still want me."

It's not dramatic. It's not a grand gesture. But it's real. It's Kevin, stripped of pretense.

I nod and pull my chair closer to his. "Tell me what happened. All of it."

Kevin does. He tells me about the first time he saw Daniel again—at Ansley outside of the gym. It was a total surprise, he says. He tells me that he gave Daniel his number so they could keep in touch, how they met up for lunch, and how they went swimming at Emory one afternoon.

My jaw tightens, but I stay quiet.

"We were just two friends catching up. That's all. He asked questions—the kind I had spent years avoiding—and I answered them. Not always immediately, nor always clearly. But I did."

"Did you have sex?"

Kevin turns, and I can see his eyes beginning to well up with tears. "No," he says immediately. "Absolutely not."

"Did the two of you kiss?" I ask, even though I already know the answer.

Kevin's elbows are resting on his knees. He raises his hands and drops his face into them, shielding himself from the question or me from the answer.

"Once," he admits. "I kissed him. I shouldn't have. Then I pulled away. It felt wrong, and I told him we shouldn't have done it."

"Because you've changed?"

"Because I've changed," he agrees.

This man I've built a life with—I study him and feel furious. Not just at him for what he's done or allowed to happen, but at myself for how much I still love him.

I don't know what I wanted—maybe a cleaner lie—something I could hate outright. Instead, Kevin gave me the truth, and now I have to decide what to do with it.

Screaming, leaving, hating—all of it tempts me. But I do none of those things.

Instead, a step forward. My hand finds the back of Kevin's head; not to hold, but to anchor us both, like someone steadying a friend who's finally stopped pretending they're fine.

"I don't need perfect," I say. "But I need honesty, and I need your presence. I need to know you're not somewhere else every time we are together. I need to stop looking at you and wondering if you're about to disappear."

Kevin's voice is barely above a whisper. "I don't want to disappear."

"Then stay," I tell him. "Stay, and we will figure it out. No more ghosts. No more silence."

Kevin nods. His eyes are glassy as tears begin to fall. He pulls me in and rests his forehead against mine.

"I'm sorry," he says.

His thumb brushes the inside of my wrist. It's a slight touch, but it tells me he's still here. We stay that way for a moment, breathing together, letting forgiveness begin to take shape. Quietly. Slowly.

"I know. So am I," I whisper back.

We don't kiss. Not yet. Instead, we sit there on the patio, hand in hand, watching the hummingbirds and butterflies do their work in the evening light, leaning into each other like two people who stop chasing closure and start choosing presence—to mend the cracks and be there for one another—and call that enough for now.

42

OUR HOME FOR THE HOLIDAYS

I t's Christmas Day, and it's been five months since I handed Josh the letter and let Kevin go. Naomi's apartment smells like cinnamon and pine—the kind of scent that settles into your clothes and follows you home. The windows fog from the stove heat and the warm breath of people who know how to love each other. Naomi stands at the stove in a red apron, one hand on her hip, the other stirring a pot of collard greens like she's conducting a symphony.

"I swear to God, Daniel," she says, pointing the wooden spoon at me, "if you slice that ham one more time like it's a vinyl bootleg, I'm going to revoke your kitchen privileges."

I hold up my hands in mock surrender. "I just believe in precision."

"You believe in control," Mateo mutters from the table, lining up forks like he's resetting a stage.

"And y'all both believe you're helping," Naomi says, "which is why I invited you early—so you could annoy each other under my supervision."

We laugh. It's easy now, the three of us. No eggshells. No subtext. Just warmth. Mateo hums along to a Smokey Robinson track playing low on the radio. Naomi sprinkles paprika over the deviled eggs with an artist's flair. The lights on the tiny tree blink in rhythm, slow and soft.

"This table looks good," I say, adjusting one last plate.

"Yeah, well," Naomi says, glancing over her shoulder, "don't get used to domesticity. I'm still wild at heart."

I lean against the counter, arms folded, watching her work. The past feels like a different apartment—not gone, just quieter. The way an old record hums beneath the groove, still spinning but no longer demanding attention.

Naomi raises an eyebrow at me. "You good? You're weirdly quiet."

"I'm good," I say, and I mean it.

She doesn't press. She nods like she believes me now.

There's a knock at the door.

Naomi hands me a towel. "Get that, would you? My hands are full."

Crossing the room, I wipe my hands dry. I know who it is, and for a second, my hand pauses on the doorknob. It's not a pause of hesitation but of anticipation.

Patrick stands in the hallway, his cheeks pink from the cold. He's wearing a slightly oversized sports coat, the kind of upscale wool thing he probably borrowed from his father's closet and thought made him look older. His hair's a little longer than the last time I saw him, falling into his eyes like he forgot to get it cut before winter break.

"Hey, stranger," I say.

"Sorry, I'm late," he says. "My mom's pecan pie held me hostage." He's holding a bottle of wine and wearing that crooked smile I remember.

He steps forward, and we hug. It's not awkward, but it is different—warmer, more familiar than flirty. We hadn't seen each other since August when he left to start his sophomore year at

Vanderbilt. Still, we'd kept in touch: a few calls, one postcard with a drawing of a turtle that made me laugh.

"Come on in," I say, stepping aside. "It's about time."

Patrick steps in, and I take his coat as he surveys the apartment. The lights are dim, the music low, and Naomi's already two glasses into the wine. Mateo's just finished lighting the last of the tea candles I scattered around the room. They emit a soft glow that makes the old apartment appear warm and festive.

"Merry Christmas, baby boy," Naomi calls from the kitchen. She appears a few seconds later and throws her arms around him. "Look at you, with that grown-up scarf and everything."

He laughs. "Trying to fool people into thinking I pay taxes."

"Well, take off your damn shoes and come grab a plate."

"Yes, ma'am," Patrick says, grinning. He glances my way, and I swear I feel the room shift—not in that dizzying way it used to when I saw Kevin across a street, but in a quiet, anchored way. Like gravity finding you.

Mateo rolls his eyes. "God, you two are insufferable." He's standing at the kitchen pass-through, arms crossed, watching with a small smile. Patrick meets his eyes and walks over, neither hurried nor hesitant. They hug. And then, in full view of all of us, Patrick leans in and kisses Mateo.

It's brief, but passionate and intentional.

No one's surprised. Not really. The two have been trading calls and letters since late summer, making vague references that turned more direct around October. Mateo mentioned Patrick more. Patrick started asking about Mateo. Naomi and I teased them once or twice, but we both knew where it was headed.

Naomi raises her glass. "Well, damn. About time."

Mateo chuckles and loops an arm casually around Patrick's waist. "We're figuring it out. Long-distance, you know. Nothing dramatic." He shrugs like it's no big deal, but the way his hand comes to rest on Patrick's back says otherwise.

I laugh. "You should've heard Patrick the night I mentioned you. Couldn't stop asking questions—what kind of music you liked, if you were seeing anyone, how tall you were."

Patrick rolls his eyes, but his grin betrays him. "You make me sound desperate."

"You were," I say, "adorably so."

Patrick shrugs, unabashed. "What can I say? I'm attracted to older guys—ones who know who they are. Mateo had that vibe from the jump. Cool. Solid. Grounded."

Naomi snorts. "Grounded? Mateo?"

She lifts her wine glass and eyes Mateo. "You're surrounded by fine-ass men at that diner and Burkhart's every night—and yet, somehow, you have to pick from the friend group?"

Mateo raises a brow. "I like quality over quantity."

Patrick nods and gives me a wink. "Exactly."

I step back and take it in—Naomi commanding the kitchen, Mateo acting unimpressed, and Patrick already barefoot like he's always belonged.

Patrick grins, then walks over to where I'm setting down a platter of roasted carrots. "This looks incredible. Did you guys cook all of this?"

"Most of it. Naomi helped. Mateo brought dessert. I worked on not burning anything," I reply.

Dinner unfolds like something we've all needed but never named: slow, unrushed conversation, second helpings, the kind of laughter that slips easily from your chest when you're full in the best way. There's no tension. No shadows. Just us.

At one point, between the ham and the pie, Naomi leans forward and says, "I may have a date next week."

Mateo raises a brow. "A date? With someone you didn't cut off in traffic or threaten to punch?"

She shrugs, half-smiling. "He's a writer. A client, technically. I'm editing his manuscript, and it's not terrible."

"That's the bar now?" I ask. "Not terrible?"

"He has strong hands and knows how to use a semicolon. I'm intrigued."

We all laugh.

Later, as we're sipping coffee and passing around whatever's left of the pecan pie, Mateo nudges me. "You didn't tell Patrick your news."

I shrug. "It's not really news yet."

Naomi squints. "Tell him."

I glance around the table, at all of them, at the flickering candles and comfort I hadn't realized had settled in my chest until now.

"Eddie and I have been talking," I say finally, "about me taking over B-Side one day."

"Daniel's been working there nights and weekends," Mateo tells Patrick.

Naomi places her fork on the table and applauds. "Our little entrepreneur."

"Not yet. But maybe someday, when Eddie's ready."

Patrick grins. "You'd own the place?"

"Maybe," I say. "I mean, I love it. I love both jobs—the best of both worlds. Pool work keeps me fit and out in the fresh air, but B-Side feels like, I don't know, my soul."

Naomi nods slowly, a smile tugging at her lips. "Sounds like someone's finally getting their shit together and building a life."

Mateo raises his glass. "To Daniel. Keeper of pools, vinyl, and vibes."

We all toast.

At last, I don't feel like I'm chasing anything. I'm not rebuilding the past or trying to become someone I'm not. I'm just here, surrounded by people I didn't have to earn or perform for. It is not the life I imagined four years ago. It's better, quieter, steadier. A little strange and a little scrappy at times—full of soft turns and sharp edges—but they don't cut like they used to.

As we sit there, full and laughing, with wine-stained lips and stories spilling over each other, I think this is what staying feels like. It's not dramatic, not perfect. But it's present, it's enough, and it's mine. I no longer feel like I'm chasing it. I'm living it.

END

THANK YOU!

I appreciate you taking the time to read my novel and hope you enjoyed the story! You are making a difference in my journey as a writer.

Please leave your honest feedback on Amazon, either by providing a star rating or writing a review. It helps me and other potential readers. You can still leave reviews on Amazon even if you obtained the book elsewhere. Reader feedback does wonders for a book, and I genuinely want to hear about your reading experience. Just scan the QR code below to leave a review:

Thank you again!

Acknowledgments

I want to express my deepest appreciation to my beta readers: **Michael Casisi, Nancy Van Fleet, David Middleton, Juan Delgado, Jackson Bass, Joey Barnes**, and **David Singleton**. Thank you for the long hours spent reading those early drafts and for your invaluable feedback.

Completing this novel wouldn't have been possible without the encouragement, mentoring, and advocacy of my best friend, **David Singleton**. A lifelong reader, library system director, and book collector extraordinaire, David never falters in his encouragement for me to continue putting words on the page while enjoying the process.

I am deeply indebted to my partner and husband, **Juan Delgado**, for his proofreading and patience as I searched for and debated that exact word to make the sentence perfect.

To my cover designer and artist, **Juan Jose Padron**. Thank you for the countless tweaks and adjustments necessary throughout the cover production process. (https://jcovers.com/)

To **Paul Myrick**. Thank you for designing, building, and maintaining my website. (https://pmyrick.com/)

LET'S STAY CONNECTED

I have many stories in the works that I look forward to sharing with you in the future. Please visit my website for a complete list of past and upcoming works. For exclusive updates and announcements, please use the QR code below to subscribe. Thank you!

https://www.djciccarello.com/

Thank you again for your support!